ONE LAST TIME

Visiting Galloway's flat in London, Inspector Merritt had an outrageous proposition to offer him: he was to go to America to steal paintings originally stolen from London's Bedford Art Gallery. Galloway could keep the huge amount of money involved, providing he could re-steal the paintings, out-smart the American police and the gangsters who had the paintings, get that money, and return to London. He accepts the challenge and manages to succeed — but not before some uncomfortably close calls.

12

MARK CARREL

---◆---

ONE LAST TIME–

Complete and Unabridged

LINFORD
Leicester

First published in Great Britain by
Robert Hale limited
London

First Linford Edition
by arrangement with
Robert Hale Limited
London
published 2006

British Library CIP Data

Carrel, Mark, *1916* –
   One last time.—Large print ed.—
Linford mystery library
1. Art thefts—Fiction
2. Detective and mystery stories
3. Large type books
I. Title
813.5′4 [F]

ISBN 1–84617–523–2

Published by
F. A. Thorpe (Publishing)
Anstey, Leicestershire

Set by Words & Graphics Ltd.
Anstey, Leicestershire
Printed and bound in Great Britain by
T. J. International Ltd., Padstow, Cornwall

This book is printed on acid-free paper

1

'Pride, Galloway, Pride.'

Inspector Merritt, a large, bulky man with a large, round face, had the appearance of a man who perspired even on cold days. It may have been simply, that no matter what he wore, worsted, tweed, or shark-skin, it always managed to look as though he had just emerged from a wrestling tag-team match, even early in the morning, as now, when he waved away the cup of tea Morton Galloway offered, hunched his great sloping shoulders over the table in Galloway's tidy little kitchen and said, 'Just one more time.'

Morton Galloway, as tall as Merritt but easily sixty pounds lighter, was also younger, although there was a hint of grey over his ears, and his smooth, tanned face, quite handsome in an aquiline way, had the expression of a man to whom most things did not come as a surprise.

1

Merritt was probably in his mid-fifties but it was never easy to be accurate about those things with large, beefy men. Galloway, on the other hand, and despite his distinguishing sprinkling of grey, was probably about forty, although with well-groomed and very careful, athletic types, it was also difficult to be sure. Galloway actually *looked* about thirty-five, but obviously, if one listened to Inspector Merritt, and if one *believed* him, Morton Galloway had to be forty-five years old, and that was a shocker because he did not really appear to be quite forty.

'You could do it,' said Merritt, watching Galloway pour himself a cup of coffee and bring it with his toast to the breakfast table. 'I can't think of another soul who could bring it off, Morton.'

Galloway stirred sweetener into his coffee, weakened it with cream, and put a jaundiced dark look on Inspector Merritt. 'Obviously, because if you could think of anyone else, Inspector, you wouldn't be here talking to me.'

Merritt looked faintly indignant. 'Not

true and you damned well know it. I'm here because you're the best at this kind of thing.'

'There must be better,' exclaimed Galloway, tasting the coffee. 'I did two years didn't I?'

Merritt brushed that aside. 'Bad bit of luck is all. We didn't have you until McComber sang his head off.'

Galloway nodded as though agreeing. 'The moral of that is always to work alone, wouldn't you say? Sure I can't get you some toast and marmalade?'

'I detest orange marmalade,' growled Inspector Merritt, and Morton Galloway looked shocked.

'That amounts to treason, you know. Well; how about tea. You don't detest tea, by any chance? What kind of an Englishman would you be, Inspector?'

Merritt had developed a very thick hide years earlier. It was very difficult to get a rise out of him with just mild teasing, and this morning in particular, he could ignore Galloway's little petards without any effort.

'No tea, thanks. Look, Galloway, it

would be quite a feather for you. And you'd have an opportunity to see the States. California, Los Angeles, Hollywood, all the places you've always . . . '

'Inspector,' said Morton Galloway, reaching for toast, 'you know perfectly well I've seen Hollywood and Los Angeles. Why else are you here this morning, than because you know I've been over there, know those places inside and out.'

Merritt waited until Galloway had chewed half-way through his toast before speaking again. 'There is quite a bit of money involved. You get to keep as much of it as you can get.'

'No thanks. Sure you won't change your mind, this is very good toast.'

'And it should be a very interesting excursion,' said Inspector Merritt.

'I could boil you an egg. Surely you haven't eaten, it's too early.'

'You'd be doing a great service, Galloway.'

'Maybe you'd prefer coffee to tea, Inspector.'

'And Mitreman is in it.'

For five seconds Morton Galloway chewed and impassively gazed across the table. Merritt fished forth a crumpled packet of cigarettes, lit one and dropped the packet as he reached for an ashtray. 'On second thoughts, I might like a cup of coffee,' he said, smiling softly.

Galloway swallowed the toast, pushed the plate aside and fixed Merritt with an unblinking stare. 'Mitreman is in it — how?'

'Well, it's his show. He's the one who set everything up.'

'You know that for a fact, do you?'

Inspector Merritt tapped ash before answering. 'If you mean can I prove it in court, of course not, but if you mean are the police sure, the answer is an unequivocal yes.'

Galloway picked up the crumpled packet, dug out a cigarette and leaned into the flash of flame Inspector Merritt held forth. He inhaled, blew smoke, and reached for his coffee again.

'From the top,' he said to Merritt. 'And Inspector, if you're using me . . . '

Merritt shrugged his wrestler's shoulders. 'Judge for yourself, Galloway. Bernard Mitreman flew over the day before the attaché case turned up, empty, from the Bedford Art Gallery. We have a description of the thief, which I'll furnish you with if you'd like, or at least a description of the man who was seen inside the gallery carrying the attaché case. The next day Mitreman flies out of Heathrow for Hollywood — Beverly Hills actually — and the following day the forgeries are identified.'

Morton Galloway blew smoke. 'Too close, Inspector. Much too close. Assuming Mitreman landed over there with his art gallery treasures, and made it all right, he had only one day to play with, and that's too close.'

Merritt was unconvinced. 'Galloway, how long would it take you to sell those things, providing someone over there knew you had them and knew you were on your way?'

Galloway shook his head. 'It's still too close. Assuming Mitreman planed out directly from New York for Los Angeles, that's an overnight flight, and assuming his contact in Beverly Hills met him at Los Angeles Municipal Airport, whisked him to Beverly Hills — a two-hour drive — and also assuming that his contact had the cash ready and waiting, it was much too close, because even if Mitreman got the money and handed over the art-work, by that evening the word would have reached over there, from here.'

Inspector Merritt nodded. 'Right enough. But having the word reach there, and being able to pick anyone up, are two quite separate things. And that is why I thought of you. McComber, remember?'

Galloway killed his cigarette in the ashtray and arose to go refill his coffee cup. 'Of course I remember; sold me out for three thousand.'

'To Mitreman,' exclaimed Merritt, and repeated it. 'Sold you out to Mitreman, Morton. Why? Because you made a very bad mistake; you stepped over the line and operated in Mitreman's territory. Melodramatic as it may sound, you stepped on someone's toes, and for that Mister Someone set you up and knocked you into my arms.'

Morton Galloway returned to the table, shot a look at his guest, and with a wide-mouthed, humourless smile, said, 'Inspector, the idea that I want a shot at Mitreman is valid. He set me up so perfectly that you didn't even have to make a case to get a conviction. But your enthusiasm to see one crook turn upon another crook doesn't quite jell with me, because, you see, I've got just as much reason to hate your guts. You're the one who sent me away, and you *knew* it was Mitreman's frame-up from the very beginning.'

Merritt did not blush. He punched out his smoke and leaned in the chair. 'Get it straightened out,' he said. 'My job is to do exactly what I did, and what you knew perfectly well I'd do the first chance I got at you. With Mitreman it was a deliberate double-cross. He set you up with McComber, and with the job you got sent over for pulling, just so that he could frame you. It was premeditated on his part from start to finish. On my part, it was nothing more and nothing less than

I've been getting paid to do for fifteen years, and you were no different to me than a hundred others, except perhaps, that you had a bit more of a reputation.' Merritt smiled. 'Not in the field of art work, which was your downfall. You never should have left the antique jewellery line of work, Morton.'

Galloway drank his second cup of coffee and looked thoughtful. 'It won't work,' he said. 'Mitreman may not know I'm out, but he'll certainly know it the moment he sees me over there.'

Merritt said, 'Why? Look about, every third or fourth man you see has a beard nowadays.'

Galloway's lip curled. 'That went out with Sherlock Holmes.'

'And it's come back, the same as Holmes has, too. Hair-dye and a beard. He hasn't seen you in a number of years, and over there, where he certainly won't be expecting to see you.' Merritt paused, then said, 'All right; there is a slight possibility that he'll recognize you. But after all, you're certainly his match, aren't you? And knowing that he might recognize you would make you that much more careful, wouldn't it?'

Galloway did not respond to that, he arose, stalked to a window that overlooked some chimney pots and dull slate, and with his back to Inspector Merritt he said, 'What, exactly, is it that you expect me to accomplish over there? After all, neither one of us will be anywhere near your jurisdiction, and even if I can get the cash he got for the stolen paintings, you nor the gallery nor the insurance people will ever see a cent of it, you know.'

Merritt arose and cast a look at his wristwatch. 'Morton, just bring back the canvases. The money is all yours. Just bring back the masterpieces.'

Galloway turned. 'How? *Steal* them, Inspector?'

Merritt smiled, adjusted the coat that fit him like last year's horseblanket, and dropped an envelope atop the cluttered breakfast table. 'A one-way ticket to Los Angeles. You'll be able to buy the return ticket out of your — proceeds.' He stood there gazing across the room at the leaner, more handsome man. 'Galloway, there are times when I'd give away five years to be able to trade places with someone. This is one of them. By the way, my home address is in that envelope. Please don't contact me unless you absolutely have to, then use the home address. And good luck. I have all the faith in the world in you.'

Galloway let Inspector Merritt get all the way to the door before he said, 'What is to prevent me, once I re-steal the art work, from disposing of it in Central America or Europe? Give me one good, sound reason why I should bring it back to London.'

Merritt opened the door and stepped through before answering. 'Pride, Galloway, pride. Good-bye and good luck.'

2

Time to Kill

Galloway was tempted to spend the balance of the day after Merritt's visit at the Bedford Art Gallery. The reason he didn't was because so soon after the shocking robbery there would be police and, worse, newsmen, on the premises. What he did not want, if he accepted Merritt's suggestion to become involved, was publicity, particularly photographic publicity in newspapers.

It wasn't necessary to go out there in any case. The newspapers had the entire story, and it was crisply simple and efficient. Art-lovers streamed through the gallery almost every day, more on rainy and cold days than otherwise. A young man, well-dressed, decently groomed, carrying an attaché case, had entered the building with about a dozen others on the previous Tuesday. He was the only person whom the guards could not afterwards say emphatically they had seen leave, but then no one asked them for two days and by then, if the attaché case hadn't been found where someone had hurled it into some shrubbery, the guards probably would not even have recalled the young man. They could very readily associate him with the case because he was the only person who entered Bedford Gallery carrying one.

The reason the police, including Inspector Merritt, felt that the attaché case was connected with the Bedford robbery was because inside it were the scalpels, the flakes of antique paint, and the gloves used by the young man. He had simply hid out in the old stone gallery until after hours, and then he'd had all night to remove the paintings for which he had forgeries in the attaché case, glue up the forgeries, put the originals in his case, and exit through any one of the ground-floor windows, and that is exactly how the police had reconstructed the crime, but only after a Bedford Gallery director, Sir James

Howard, made the horrifying discovery that no less than six valuable paintings had been made off with.

The police did not give a figure for the loss, and the Bedford Gallery directors declined to do so on private grounds, which left it up to some enterprising newsman. He did his research rather well and came up with a nice, round figure. If, he wrote, the paintings went to the Continent, they would bring a lorryload of escudos, pesos, liras, francs and reichsmarks. If they went to America they would probably fetch a half a million dollars, and if they went to the Orient — Hong Kong or Shanghai — they would probably be snapped up at a savings by either the Soviet Union or the People's Republic of China, kept a few years, then be allowed to surface in some place like Budapest or Poznan, offered for sale to the West at approximately a half million dollars, U.S., the money then going into the Soviet or Chinese war coffers.

Galloway read all this and sipped coffee, and smiled to himself because although, it was said repeatedly that the robbery had occurred too recently for the police to have made any progress, Inspector Merrit was proof to the contrary. Galloway should have pressed for the details on how the police had turned up the facts so swiftly. Ordinarily, they didn't do this. Ordinarily, the police were slow, redundant, dogged, and unenlightened — but ultimately successful.

He speculated about the young man. Of course he wasn't important, and Galloway knew the procedure Bernard Mitreman used, it did not vary nor was there any reason for it to; Mitreman was always successful, and if anyone got caught it was the McCombers, or the young men with the attaché cases, but it was never Bernard Mitreman. As Merritt had once said, 'You cannot put a hand upon someone who has not been within miles of a crime when it's been committed, and complicity under those circumstances is impossible to prove. The trouble is that nowadays criminals know more law than lawyers know.'

Galloway's own difficulty with Bernard

Mitreman had occurred roughly three years before. Galloway, whose speciality was antique jewellery, had had an opportunity to join with a man named McComber in raiding an art gallery. It had looked so simple, and in fact the actual robbery had been very simple and very successful, until McComber went to the police. He had been hired by Mitreman to frame Morton Galloway, the newcomer, the upstart, the smart-alec who didn't have sense enough to stay in his own rut. With two years to think about it, Galloway had come out feeling vindictive, but more than that, feeling smarter. If Inspector Merritt hadn't come along, Galloway would have gone after Mitreman on his own. That was what he had dwelt upon at considerable length while in prison, and after two years a man has to arrive at some rather definite conclusions.

Galloway knew *what* he was going to do to Bernard Mitreman, but until Merritt came along, he hadn't been very sure just *how* he would do it. On the other hand, he had no intention of allowing Inspector Merritt — the enemy — to know one bit more than was absolutely necessary. Nor had Galloway been joking when he'd asked why he should bring the stolen art work back to England. He hadn't made up his mind what to do with it, immediately after his visit from Merritt, but as he sat drinking coffee, reading the newspapers, and gradually learning to approve of what he had become involved in, he decided that Inspector Merritt had been correct: Pride would make him return the art work to Bedford Gallery.

Merritt's envelope with the one-way reservation to Los Angeles Municipal Airport also contained a slip of paper with Merritt's residential address and telephone number, but not his name, and that was all it contained, so Galloway had to get dressed for the street, go visit his bank to withdraw as much money as he thought would be needed even for a high-roller in Beverly Hills, the rich-man's suburb of Los Angeles, then he went to his favourite public establishment, bought the latest newspapers and re-read as much as was known about the Bedford Gallery robbery.

There was no mention of the young man who had stolen the paintings, and that annoyed Morton Galloway. Either the police had him or they didn't have him. Either way they were not very explicit, at least the newspapers side-stepped mentioning this matter, so Galloway finally went to a telephone and called Merritt. The Inspector said, 'These things take time,' and Morton Galloway said, 'Don't be like that to me, Inspector. To the press, as you wish, but I'm involved, remember? If this man is likely to be over there, too, I'd like to know.'

Merritt paused to sigh. 'Well, we know who he is, but frankly he's somewhere on the Continent and although there is a dragnet out and I'm confident of getting him eventually, right now, at this moment, I have no idea where he might be.'

'So,' said Galloway, 'he could have gone all the way on Air Italia or Air France.'

Merritt concurred. 'Possibly, yes, but we have the Mitreman pattern, Galloway. It has never before included an additional association between the master and the novice. Basically, Mitreman knows that police contact must come through the man who does the actual robbery. If he has absolutely no contact after acquiring the art work, if he goes to America while the robber goes to the Continent, there can't be a connection can there? Frankly, I doubt very much that the thief will show up in California. I have a private feeling that if he did, he'd be doing it voluntarily, perhaps with something like a shake-down in mind, and for anyone who might try that with Mitreman I have sympathy.'

Galloway rang off, satisfied, and returned to his flat to spend the last hours of his comfortable existence making, and rejecting, plans. He did not own a gun. It was not a very good idea to own one in Britain. In America he could saunter down the street in Los Angeles and buy one without much difficulty. The possibility that a gun might be necessary crossed his mind very naturally. In America when someone got involved in something like

Galloway was contemplating, there was an excellent possibility that the opposition would overreact.

Galloway did not ordinarily think in terms of weapons.

A good thief did not very often use, or need, weapons. His best tool was his intelligence. But in a country where intelligent thieves seldom talked their way past unintelligent gunmen, it was a good idea to go prepared.

Otherwise, Galloway did not take Inspector Merritt's suggestion of the beard and hair-dye. He had an idea that he would have done whatever had to be accomplished long before he could grow a beard. Also, as he remembered conservative, rich and luxurious Beverly Hills, beards, shaggy hair, bell-bottomed trousers and the like would make someone stand out. What Galloway had always prided himself upon was his ability to be almost completely inconspicuous. In his profession, the theft of valuable antique jewellery, anonymity was absolutely essential. It would probably be as essential in the stealing, or the *re*-stealing, of Bedford Gallery's art work.

Another encouraging element in all this, was that the stolen paintings, six in number, were not Picassos nor Cézannes; they were of course listed in catalogues, and they were valuable, otherwise no one would have stolen them, but they were *moderately* valuable, not excessively valuable. In short, they were the kind of paintings that not one person out of a thousand had ever heard of, except in the art world. They were what dealers called 'investment hedges', they probably would become valuable some day, and as inflation spiralled their value would increase correspondingly, so if someone desired to get into the art-collection business for about half a million dollars, he could do it with what Bernard Mitreman had to offer. But of course Mitreman hadn't had the paintings stolen because he, personally, had them to offer; Mitreman would operate through an art dealer. He probably would sell his paintings outright, at a discounted figure.

Morton Galloway guessed that Mitreman might have to take as little as a quarter of a million dollars for his stolen works of art. If one considered Mitreman's time — one flight to California, one flight back to London — and his capital outlay for the flight, for his hotel and his meals and perhaps for his rented car, a fair estimate of Mitreman's profit would be probably in the neighbourhood of two hundred and forty-seven thousand dollars, or, on an hourly basis, many times over what the Prime Minister and President got, combined.

Galloway had one particular problem. He did not really know Bernard Mitreman. The man was a sort of international wraith, and while this did not especially trouble Galloway, what *did* bother him was Mitreman's behaviour after he got his money for the stolen art work. Would he fly back to London, would he decide to travel, perhaps to Greece and lie in the sun, or would he, having read about the discovery of the robbery, decide to stay right where he was, in expensive but very comfortable, Beverly Hills?

Galloway did not have unlimited funds. He could not rely on any from Inspector

Merritt. He could afford to make the flight to Beverly Hills — Los Angeles, actually — and he could afford to sustain himself in solid comfort for a month or so, but if Mitreman wasn't over there, if he had quietly dropped from sight, Galloway was not going to be able to bank-roll himself for the length of time a concerted search would require.

Merritt had handed Galloway a hot potato, had helped get him started with that one-way flight ticket, and now Galloway, with his inherent gambler's instincts, had taken the bait.

Of course, if he should happen to be successful, then *his* hourly rate would exceed that of the combined income of the President and the P.M. The problem was that he not only had to find Bernard Mitreman and positively identify him, he also had to loot him down to his socks, and Mitreman's reputation was good enough to make this kind of an undertaking shade hell out of the odds. Galloway stood at a window in his flat watching the street below, thinking that on balance, what had looked like good odds when Merritt had been there that morning, by late afternoon looked like not just fifty-fifty odds, but maybe even sixty-forty odds, in Mitreman's favour.

Galloway smiled to himself. A resourceful man, with enough ego to believe he was just about anyone's match, probably wouldn't die of old age anyway.

He left the window, went after a suitcase and began pitching the things he thought he would need over in Beverly Hills into it. Whatever else he might need over there he would walk down the street in Los Angeles's pawnbrokers district and buy, complete with a nice, smooth, shoulder-holster. If Mitreman beat him again, at least Mitreman was going to know he'd been in a ball game.

3

The Too-Easy Sequence

It might have been considered a bad omen if Galloway had been omen-conscious, but his flight was diverted from Los Angeles Municipal Airport to Portland, Oregon, Municipal Airport. Los Angeles had just suffered from perhaps the most devastating earthquake in its history and the airport runways had cracks and buckled places that made any kind of landing dangerous.

From Oregon, Galloway took a milk-run flight down to Sacramento, and from there he rode a Greyhound bus to Los Angeles, entering the city in a discreet, somewhat seamy manner.

He got back out to Beverly Hills by private car, put up at a hotel he remembered from a previous visit as being an especially swinging pad, and did nothing but bathe and loaf for the first full day after his arrival, allowing the psychological clock inside his head to make the nine-hour adjustment. Not that he was tired or sleepy; he just did not feel as though morning should have arrived when it did.

The following day he went forth to quickly renew an old acquaintanceship with Beverly Hills, which actually was a rather old community, as California communities went, dating from the opulent days of silent movies, when income taxes had been low, incomes exorbitantly high, and laws, like morals, conspicuously lax.

Movie people had made Beverly Hills, and after their gradual decline, industrialists moved in, many supported by the new glamour-field, called aerospace, but whatever pumped the green blood into Beverly Hills, it took wealth to live there, although now there were many more people, leech-like, who looked and acted the part, but who actually had little or no wealth of their own and whose speciality was trying to cadge a living off those who had money.

Galloway decided the place hadn't changed much. On his previous visit, six years earlier, he had had a salutary association with a man named Max Levine — pronounced La Von — but no one in Levine's neighbourhood even remembered him now, which was probably just as well since Galloway did not want anyone around who would know him.

There had been a long-stemmed American Beauty too, but their wilt-prone capacity made it highly improbable that she would still be around. Still, Galloway went out to make certain of that, too. He wanted, above all else, to be just another face in the crowd. Whatever happened, he didn't want anyone popping up from six years back identifying him.

The long-legged girl was not even a memory.

Galloway bought a new suit and got his sideburns put back up where they belonged, hired a car and set about very systematically, with the aid of the Yellow Pages of the telephone directory, acquainting himself with every art dealer in Beverly Hills. There was a staggering number of them, because Beverly Hills had expanded a little since his last visit, and now included the Hebrew barriors south, east, and west, of where the original boundary lines were.

Probably one-third of those dealers could be eliminated after one pass out front of their stores, because they obviously were too small. They might have an excellent and very select clientele, but Galloway was ruthless; if they obviously operated on a moderate budget they would not have the kind of cash it would take to handle the Mitreman deal.

That left a better-class variety of store, closer, in fact, to the green heart of Beverly Hills, and these shops were staid, quiet, quite elegant in fact and just looking at them would never be enough. On the other hand making a personal canvass could be fatal, later, if Galloway found what he sought, because in the event of a robbery the Beverly Hills police, like the London police, would ask the same questions: Who was here asking about paintings before the robbery?

What Galloway wanted was anonymity. He also wanted to know which art dealer Mitreman had contacted. It was, he told himself, like establishing a goal for one's self, then establishing a dozen insurmountable obstacles to that goal.

He smiled and went to dinner the second day in a smart little Hungarian restaurant where the wine was served room-temperature, a rarity in California where even the beer was served almost without exception, so cold it was difficult to drink it.

He had narrowed down his consideration of the art galleries to those in the exclusive and very expensive heart of Beverly Hills. Nor had he actually thought right from the start that what he sought would turn up anywhere else, but Galloway was a thorough, as well as a very shrewd, man.

What he had to do next was find Mitreman.

A buxom waitress who would have a downy, dark moustache by the time she was thirty, came to lean and ask if Galloway cared for more wine. He entertained one fleeting thought about her, then rejected it along with her offer of wine. There was an awful lot of money at stake. There was also a fair possibility that someone's life — his own — might be at stake sooner or later. Those were considerations that tended to dampen a lot of ardour, tended to dull a lot of lovely rounded vistas.

The third day Galloway was in Beverly Hills he devoted to suave deceit and straight-faced lying. If he had been a policeman he would not have needed to resort to either, but he was not, and had never entertained any desire to be a policeman, although that was part of his deception when he made one telephone call after another identifying himself as a detective connected with the Bureaux of Missing Persons seeking information on a man, probably using a name like Mittle-man or Michaels or Michelin, who had flown in out at Municipal Airport the previous Tuesday or Wednesday from New York, but whose original ticket-stub would have shown London to be the source of his trip.

The only encouragement he got was from a young clerk who could not have been a native because he was too polite and too helpful. This person remembered a Mister Mitreman, if that would be of any help, whose point of origin had been London, flying in the previous Wednesday from New York, and who had the clerk call him a taxi to take him to the Beverly-Hilton Hotel. The clerk remembered the name of the hotel because Mr Mitreman had not looked like a Beverly-Hilton candidate.

Galloway was ever so grateful. Afterwards, he went out to buy some cigarettes, and to make a brisk promenade for exercise, and later to enter one of the delightful little parks that abounded in Beverly Hills, and have a seat beneath a mammoth old palm tree while he pondered the means to be employed in finding which suite at the Hilton had a Mitreman in it, and to also speculate on the conceit of a man who, although involved in a robbery, scorned an alias and went blithely about his business as though the police on two continents could not make a shred of trouble for him. Mitreman was a worthy opponent.

Galloway saw the beautiful legs coming towards him through the little park before he saw anything else. He was a man who enjoyed sleek lines on ships, horses, aeroplanes and women.

The beautiful legs went past, Galloway did not look despite an almost over-whelming urge to do so, and put out his cigarette as he arose to stroll back the way he had come.

He was beginning to have a vague feeling that Fate was setting him up; that locating Mitreman was turning out to be far too easy.

He returned to his quarters, considered calling for Mitreman at the Hilton to get the number of his suite, decided that was moving in too quickly and too close, and waited until about sundown to change, shower, and go back downstairs to the car he'd rented. The drive over to the Beverly-Hilton on Wilshire Boulevard took only moments. The day-long tangle of traffic was minimal at dinner-time.

Even finding a parking place, to Galloway's surprise, was easy, and that made him more than ever conscious that all this was turning out to be much too easy.

Somewhere up ahead there was one hell of a bump.

Every underground garage had two shifts of attendants, day and night, and Galloway's approach to the husky youth he met in the concrete bunker where the Hilton's guests left their cars, while not in the least sympathetic with someone from a finance company come to perhaps repossess a vehicle, was not above accepting a ten-dollar note for looking up the slot where a guest named Mitreman parked.

There was a large plot in the attendant's office showing every car by the number assigned to the guest who left it. Mitreman's number was 4122. 'Four,' explained the youth, 'because that's the floor, 122, because that's the number of his diggings on the fourth floor. Get it?'

Galloway smiled. 'Very simple and sound system,' he said. 'Thanks.'

The youth stepped out and pointed.

'Follow that aisle and watch the numbers after one hundred. This guy's car'll be round the bend down there.'

The directions were correct, but Galloway didn't want to see the car, he'd only meant to use it to find out which suite upstairs housed Bernard Mitreman.

'Much too easy,' he told the parked car, when he found it and verified that it had been leased to one Bernard Mitreman by the second largest renter of cars in Los Angeles.

The car was dark, moderately heavy, and a year or two old. It was exactly the kind of a car anyone preferring not to attract attention would want. In fact, Morton Galloway's rented car, although of a different make, was in all other respects a perfect image of Mitreman's car.

He left the garage, saw that dusk was settling in earnest, and took a long chance by going into the hotel, riding a lift to the fourth floor, and pausing a moment in front of Suite 122 while he heard music beyond the door, for as long as it took to re-tie a shoe. Mitreman was at home. The gamble was whether he would stay in this evening or go out. Galloway consulted his watch and decided that Mitreman would go out, unless he did not eat dinner for some personal reason, because it was that time.

There was a possibility that Mitreman had already eaten. Galloway considered his luck up until now, decided that Mitreman had *not* eaten, and went along the carpetted corridor to a distant window where there was a small, curtained-off maintenance closet, and decided to allow Mitreman a half-hour to leave.

He had to know what his man looked like. He knew enough other things about Mitreman, but without being able to recognize him those other things were useless.

He smoked a cigarette, looked down where shadows were puddling over Wilshire Boulevard, where cars were beginning to materialize and multiply, and wondered if, by any chance, his luck was going to hold long enough for everything to work out. If it did, he would be back in London by the end of the week.

If it were true that every artisan had a special guardian deity, then the one who cared for the interests of men whose profession had been the theft of antique jewellery was especially active in California, in the springtime, because when Galloway was leaning to kill his cigarette in a sand-filled ornate urn, the door to Suite 122 opened, a rather thickset, swarthy man emerged, locked the door after himself, shot a look up and down the corridor, then shuffled over to a mechanical lift and punched the button.

Galloway finished putting out his cigarette, sighed to himself, and sauntered down the corridor for a second look at Bernard Mitreman just as the shorter, thicker man entered the lift and the door began to close. Mitreman, strangely enough, looked Italian, and he also looked physically powerful in the same way that a beer-barrel was powerful. Then the doors closed, the lift sank, and Galloway went without haste to the stairway.

When he reached the lobby Mitreman was nowhere in sight. Galloway thought of going to stand near the garage exit, but decided that was unnecessary. He knew his man; would know him the next day when he took up the trail. Sooner or later Mitreman would lead Galloway to the dealer who had bought the art work, and that would signify that two-thirds of Galloway's work in America was finished.

He returned to his own hotel, bought a couple of local newspapers at the desk, and took them upstairs to read. They would be very poor substitutes for the buxom waitress in the Hungarian restaurant, or for the fabulously racy pair of legs in the little park, but newspapers never got one otherwise very involved, either.

Later, because he intended to be across from the Hilton early enough to pick up his man if Mitreman should turn out to be an early-bird, Galloway turned in early without even remembering to turn on the colour television set in his quarters.

4

The End of the Run of Luck

Beverly Hills had two standards for early
morning risers. One, they padded out in
slippers and robes to get the morning
paper just in case a war had started while
they had slept, then padded back
gloomily into their houses and hotel
suites, or, two, they bounced out dressed
expertly and ready to go forth and daunt
the world.

Galloway did neither. He parked his
rented car across from Mitreman's hotel,
lit a cigarette, turned on the dashboard
radio, got comfortable, and waited. His
private guess was that Bernard Mitreman
would not be an early-bird, but on the
other hand what harm could come from
making certain?

An hour later, with traffic as thick as
the lamenting hordes of the Exodus,
Galloway deciding he might miss his

man, left the car to cross the street and go take up a secluded position beneath an unkempt elm tree in a private parkway where he commanded a good view of the garage's exit.

By ten o'clock he was prepared to accept as fact that either Mitreman had somehow eluded him, which was unlikely, or that Mitreman was a sloth who did not greet daylight until noon.

While he was deciding which of those options to accept, it occurred to him that he might have a third option. As a thoroughly accomplished and sophisticated burglar, he might conceivably expedite the issue that currently interested him — locating which art dealer Mitreman had done business with — by getting inside Suite 122 and perhaps rummaging some suit-pockets or some luggage.

If Mitreman were there, Galloway would not disturb him, unless it was absolutely necessary, but if he were *not* there, then his having eluded Galloway might be compensated for by whatever Galloway could turn up.

He crossed the street, went briskly to the main entranceway of the hotel, which was a pair of very massive brass-and-glass doors, entered the lobby where it was fifteen degrees cooler than it was outside, and mingled with the crowd all the way to the lifts.

On the fourth floor he encountered two couples waiting to descend, to whom he abandoned his lift, and, not so convenient, he also encountered a clean-up crew of two coloured women whom he had to get around to approach Mitreman's door. There was an abrupt turn in the hallway leading towards that window where Galloway had stood the evening before. He went down there, hoisted the window, stepped out upon the fire-escape, moved carefully along it to a window belonging to Suite 122, used his fist wrapped in an Irish linen handkerchief to crush the glass below the hasp, reached in to lift the window, and within moments was standing in the sitting-room of Suite 122, which was not quite elaborate, but which was considerably more elaborate than Galloway's sitting-room at the other hotel he had access to.

There was a feel of emptiness to the suite. People, other than thieves and burglars, were attuned to emptiness in rooms, but burglars usually developed a very excellent ability to sense this emptiness over the years. Galloway glided across the room, lifted the latch on the door which was standard precautionary procedure — in case one had to leave hurriedly — then he turned and made a slow, thoughtful survey of the sitting-room, at the same time wondering how he could have missed Mitreman downstairs.

The sitting-room had hardly been used. Galloway went over to a short, gloomy little corridor and saw the closed door. Beyond, of course, was the bedroom. He was still not willing to admit that Mitreman had eluded him, so, as he approached the closed door, he loosened his coat. In the event a man had to strike someone down, fast, it could best be accomplished without the constriction of a buttoned jacket. On the other hand, if

Mitreman the sloth was still abed in there, Galloway would probably be able to ransack his jacket and trouser-pockets without much trouble. Sleeping men were rarely ever awakened by professional break-and-enter men.

It took a moment to guess which way to apply his body weight to prevent the bedroom door from squeaking when it was opened. Downward, because the hinges were on the right side, or with their spindles pointing upwards.

Galloway got the door open, saw the gloom where drawn draperies kept out that delightful Southern California sunshine, and also made out the great lump under the covers of the bed.

He approached the bed from behind, slid a hand beneath the pillow looking for the gun, and when he did not find it he decided that Bernard Mitreman, like Galloway, just was not up to it because of the homeland environment. He then looked for the clothing that he expected to find over the back of a chair, but which were actually hanging very properly in a closet with the door open.

Galloway had to cross the front of the bed to reach that closet. His back would be to the face of the man in the bed. He did not expect Mitreman to awaken but he hesitated to take that chance. Finally willing to do this, because he had to, and because he was so tantalizingly close to what most certainly was the end of the trail that procrastination at this point would be utterly destructive, Galloway stepped around without a sound, kept an eye towards the still lump in the bed, and reached to lift out the clothes. He was masterfully successful. There was not even the scrape of metal hanger over wood when he lifted the clothing and stepped away, off to one side out of the sleeping man's view.

The first shock was when he discovered that the trouser pockets had been pulled inside out. The second shock came when he discovered that everything superfluous, like Mitreman's handkerchief, his holder containing a comb and nail file, his small change, was scattered over the rug underfoot, and Galloway's final shock came when it dawned on him where he was and what was facing him.

He very gently put the clothing aside, stepped up to the bedside table and flicked on the light. Then, finally, he saw the malevolent pair of dry brown eyes staring at him. This was *not* the man he had seen leaving the apartment last night — and *this man was dead*!

Galloway stepped back as far as a chifferobe and fished for his cigarettes, lit one and stood there considering the fat, swarthy face lying so comfortably upon the pillow.

It didn't actually matter how that corpse had become one, and it didn't actually matter very much to Galloway that instinct told him that he was looking at the man he might even have killed, himself, if circumstances had been right. What mattered now was that Fate was having her big loud laugh about now. She had let him be so successful at sleuthing that he had actually thought he might be winging his way homeward by the end of the week.

He remembered thinking that some-where up ahead was a big jolt. Well; here it was. He blew smoke at the unblinking dark eyes that stared directly at him, and decided that what should have been near to its conclusion by the end of the week, was probably going to be just beginning.

He ransacked the room and found nothing helpful, but of course that other man, the Italian-looking one he had seen leave the apartment last night, the man who had killed Mitreman, would already have anything of value.

Galloway went back out into the bright and normal sitting-room. That gloomy bedroom with its cooling contents did not do much for his equanimity. He finished his smoke, killed it, pocketed the butt and stepped back through the window to the fire-escape. Far below Beverly Hills with its sedate residential areas and their great trees, their lane after lane of date palms, seemed too orderly and decorous to countenance murder. He smiled crookedly, ducked into the corridor, which was empty, and locked the window at his back before going to the lift.

No one saw him leave, but of course there were those people to whom he had relinquished his lift, and there were also the cleaning people, who had seen him up there on the fourth floor. Trust the police to get a description of him. As he left the lift in the lobby and went among the crowd again heading for the streetside doors, he wished for the first time that he had listened to Inspector Merritt's corny idea of the beard and dyed hair.

And of course the police were going to discover the broken window where Galloway gained entrance, back there. That, he thought, as he crossed to his parked car, was not going to upset the police as much as it was going to upset that Italian-looking man who had really done the killing, when he read about it in the newspapers. He was going to be very puzzled, since he obviously had entered the suite by the front door.

Galloway got into his rented car and sat perfectly still for a moment. If Mitreman had opened the door to the squatty, dark man, and if Mitreman had invited him into the suite, then Mitreman had known him, or at least had been expecting him to call.

Galloway drove slowly and circuitously back to his hotel, put up the car and went upstairs to shower and change into cotton trousers and polo shirt. He would have paid five times over for a chilled gin and tonic, but for the time being that was out; he had no mix and he was not going to get redressed just to go hunt up a bar where he could sit and drink, while he thought. He would be able, or so it was commonly said, to think much more clearly without any stimulant.

Beginning at the top, he knew who the killer was. That is, he would recognize him on sight. Also, since obviously the killer had not chosen to telephone the police, no one knew Mitreman was dead. Not yet, and that also gave Galloway some kind of illusive and probably very temporary advantage. Finally, Mitreman's murder, patently related to robbery since his personal effects had been cleaned out right down to the wallet itself, was very clearly not a case of a random burglary and subsequent murder, otherwise Mitreman's papers would also have been flung on the floor, just his money taken.

Galloway decided to go after that drink after all. He got dressed and went out into the sunlight, and instead of using the car, he walked a good long mile to find the place he sought. It had to be quiet, gloomy, not very popularly patronized around midday, and with a bartender who did not try to push drinks.

Galloway took his tall gin and tonic to a corner table where it was as dark as early evening, sat down, relaxed, sipped his highball, and decided that the Italian-looking man might be an art dealer, or he might be the muscle employed by an art dealer, but in either case, the barrel-shaped killer probably had been sent to take care of Mitreman so that someone, possibly himself, would not have to pay out something between a quarter and a half million dollars.

People were being shot, stabbed, pushed out of private airplanes, run over, clubbed and poisoned every day of the year for an awful lot less money.

In a way it was ironic that Bernard

Mitreman whom the police on two continents had never been able to lay a hand on, lay dead because he had been clever enough to bring stolen paintings into America before anyone in London knew they had been stolen, and dispose of them, then, presumably, had to pay with his life because he had either collected a fortune in cash, or was supposed to collect a fortune in cash.

Galloway finished his drink and made two decisions. One, he would go down to the pawnbroker's area of Los Angeles the next day and buy that gun he'd thought of, and two, he would go over all the names of art dealers for an Italian name. The first thing would probably be a wise move, the second undertaking was just as probably going to be a dud.

Otherwise, there was another way he might be able to find that Italian again; at least find out who he was. He paid for his gin-and-tonic, decided that the do-gooder who said drink muddled a man's brains didn't know his up from his down, and briskly walked back to the hotel where he got comfortable again in his cotton trousers and shirt, then sat down to draw a fair likeness of the Italian upon the front page of a newspaper he had read, write beneath the likeness who the man was, fold the thing and insert it into a plain envelope and mail it to the Beverly Hills Police Department.

After that he decided to wait until the cool of night to mail the letter, and sat back wondering if, by now, someone hadn't entered Mitreman's suite — probably a cleaning woman — to have the unmitigated gumption frightened completely out of them.

Of course, if the police used his drawing to seek out a killer without letting the press in on it, or if the press was not enterprising enough to ferret out who the suspect was, and name him in a newspaper, then Galloway was no better off than before. But he had faith in the American newspaper system. Even in war-time it never neglected to tell everything it knew.

5

A Matter of Suspects

There was a new law since Galloway's last visit to the States regarding the purchase of hand-guns. He was supposed to give a résumé of his past, have his finger-prints taken, explain why he needed a revolver, and swear under oath before a notary that he had no police record. All of this would have taken most of the morning to accomplish, but the pawnbroker from whom Galloway bought the .38 revolver with its reinforced three-inch barrel, and the adjustable shoulder-holster that fit it, was conscious of the value of a customer's time. For an additional one hundred dollars he assured Galloway most solemnly that he would take care of all the legal requirements.

That made the gun rather expensive, but on the other hand it also gave Galloway a gun of which there was no trace, because obviously the pawnbroker had not registered its serial number when he had acquired the gun, and would not register the number now that he had sold the gun. It made for an expensive but neat and orderly transaction. Galloway paid the one hundred dollars then drove leisurely back to his hotel in Beverly Hills, which was no mean accomplishment in itself, traversing the full westerning distance of the largest and most car-clotted city in the entire U.S.A.

And it was hot again. Springtime in other parts of the world was a pure blessing, a complete joy to the senses and the pores. In Southern California, which was basically a sand-desert although that was difficult to discover now, with pavement and houses covering practically every inch of ground, desert heat began in February and did not diminish until the following January, with some kind of panting apex being achieved between June and September. That, in itself, would not have been so awful if it had just been desert heat, but the healthy desert dryness was overwhelmed by a sticky, oily kind of cloying smog that clogged the pores. The only way to be liberated from this unclean sweatiness was to bathe often. Galloway did, when he got back to his hotel. It was his second shower since morning and the day was slightly more than half spent. Then he redressed and went downstairs to buy the newspapers and take them to a quiet corner of the lobby, and look through for something he thought he might be a bit premature about, the identification of the Italian-looking murderer.

There was nothing in the newspapers about the Italian, but there was a front-page item about the discovery of a dead man at the Beverly-Hilton. Evidently the paper had gone to press before Mitreman's identification had been made. All the article said was that a guest had been found dead in his bed, conceivably the victim of a heart attack.

Galloway smiled. It was indeed a heart attack. The kind that was induced. He took the papers upstairs with him, sat at the little spindle-legged desk in his parlour to pen a note to Inspector

Merritt, and enclosed the clipping about the dead man in the hotel over on Wilshire Boulevard. He told Merritt all he knew. Later, when he went out to eat, he posted the letter. Later, he stopped at a liquor store for some mix and gin and took them both back to his rooms for a nightcap before turning in. He slept like a baby and awakened very refreshed the next morning. It was another of those dazzling, delicate new days that by ten o'clock would be completely devastated by the greasy grey smog riding the westerly breezes out of the industrial gut of the city.

Galloway went out for coffee and a roll, bought a newspaper and got his reward. Mitreman had been identified by name and point of origin — England — but if the police knew more, knew his record in Europe, they had not divulged it to the press. Also, it was stated that according to the coroner's preliminary report, Mr Mitreman had died from a small-calibre bullet through the heart at quite close range. The death, it was thought, had occurred at about five or six in the late afternoon, of the night before the body was discovered.

Also, there was a clue to the identity of the killer supplied by someone the police either could not, or would not, identify at this time, in the form of a letter mailed the previous evening and postmarked at one of the Beverly Hills Post Office sub-stations. From all this the newsman who had written the article Galloway read, had deduced that the killing was an exclusive Beverly Hills affair.

Galloway agreed, and folded the paper to finish his coffee and roll. He had hoped the killer's name would have been listed, but perhaps it was a bit early. He became reconciled to an all-day wait. Surely the evening papers would have the killer's name. There was nothing he could do until he learned the name, but one more wasted day wasn't going to be too unsettling, except that, as he left the restaurant, it occurred to him that he might use it to advantage by moving to another hotel. Assuming the police would be unable to trace his letter any closer than that sub-station where the stamp had been cancelled, a wise person did not underestimate even American police-men. One Englishman was dead. A routine canvass of local hotels would turn up another Englishman — Gallo-way — a discreet enquiry to London for the background of both Englishmen would turn up the fact that Mitreman had railroaded Galloway, and bingo! the Beverly Hills Police Department would have a very good suspect to book into jail on a charge of homicide.

When Galloway packed and checked out, he drove closer to, not farther from, the Beverly-Hilton Hotel, and took quarters in a duplex on North Canon Drive in a quiet, shady neighbourhood where the residences were early Mary Pickford in architecture, immaculate, and with perfectly groomed grounds. Since all were two storeys high it was hard to decide which were private residences and which were duplexes. There were immense shade trees along each parkway, and in most of the yards, so the effect was of cool shade all day long.

Galloway got settled in handily enough, put up his rented car, changed into casual, sports attire, and went walking. He had never lived anywhere that he hadn't taken the first opportunity to become thoroughly familiar with the entire neighbourhood, unless it had been those two years he'd spent under lock and key, and in that place they had discouraged brisk and exploratory walks.

He enjoyed a late luncheon and because his new home had a tiny kitchen, shopped at a supermarket then returned to the apartment with a bag of groceries, and the early edition of the evening newspaper.

His faith in American newsmen was vindicated, finally. The suspect mentioned earlier by the police was said by the reporter whose article Galloway read, to be one Anthony Martinelli, but there was now a second suspect, name unknown, whose description, given by two coloured cleaning ladies and two couples who had seen him on the fourth floor, and who was now known not to be a resident of the Beverly-Hilton Hotel, was reasonably accurate.

This man, six feet tall, about one hundred and seventy-five pounds in weight, tanned, physically fit looking, slightly grey over the ears, rather handsome and distinguished looking, with light-brown hair and grey eyes, was thought to be somewhere between thirty-five and forty-five years in age.

Galloway lit a cigarette, re-read his description, and thought that the casual look he had got from those cleaning ladies, and those two couples to whom he'd given his lift, had been unusually keen and observant. He also speculated on whether or not it was too late to accept Inspector Merritt's suggestion for the hair-dye and the beard. Not for the hair-dye, but unless he could buy a beard it was now much too late to grow one. On the other hand he was not particularly worried. That description would undoubtedly fit hundreds of local men. Also, as the police investigation progressed, it would inevitably become more and more involved with Anthony Martinelli.

Galloway went after a telephone directory. He discovered that although Beverly Hills had at least thirty Martinellis, fourteen of whom had the given name of Anthony, not a one of them was listed among the names of local art dealers. Of course that did not necessarily mean this particular Anthony Martinelli was not a dealer; many of the art salons were listed by the name of the store, or the company, not with any individual names listed.

Galloway entered his small kitchen to make himself a drink. He now had two problems. The first one, his apprehension by the police, did not bother him very much, although he knew that if he stayed around very long they would certainly come for him; back-tracking was easy enough. It would not take very many days for them to discover that *two*, not just one, Englishmen, had entered Los Angeles, within the past week or so. And for all Galloway knew there may have been a dozen or more others, as well. But narrowing it down to the Beverly Hills area would not be difficult. Two Englishmen had rented cars in Beverly Hills within the past ten days and now one of them was dead. Routine interest would do the rest, plus a line-up with Galloway in it for the coloured cleaning ladies and those two couples to identify.

It did not really worry him too much. Not because he felt serenely innocent of murder, in his heart, but because he estimated that it would take the police three more days at the least to identify Galloway, and with just a little luck he ought to be well along towards what he'd come here to do, by then, now that he knew who the killer was.

By Galloway's revised schedule he had one day to locate Anthony Martinelli, one day to find out who he worked for, or if he worked for himself, where he had the stolen art work cached, and one day — probably the most touch-and-go of the lot — to plane out for home.

He decided that it might be a good idea not to wait until the following morning to start his manhunt. While there was still daylight he undertook a canvass of the art shops. Sometimes, there were names in gold print on the doors or windows. One of the most difficult aspects of human ego to suppress was the compulsion to see one's name in gold-leaf upon a door or window.

It was not beginning to cool very much when Galloway drove into the heart of Beverly Hills, parked in a quiet sidestreet, and began his sauntering. He had hoped for a little breeze. Usually, because the city was actually only a few miles from the Pacific Ocean, there was a cooling trend in the afternoon. Not today; the heat boiled up from all that unrelieved pavement, bounded back off plate-glass shop windows, and quivered like jelly from the fronts of all the side-by-side buildings. The only advantage with pedestrians lay in the fact that as the sun sank in the west, if they took that same side of the streets, at least they found hot shade instead of hot sunlight. Galloway could not always do that; not every art dealer's salon was on the west side of the street.

He knew most of the exhibition rooms from having previously cruised past in his rented car. He was also aware of some slight peril each time he paused to look at the art displays and search for names. The Beverly Hills police, by now, undoubtedly knew that Mitreman had been an art dealer. They would be concentrating upon dealers and dealers' salons. They would also be concentrating, perhaps, on anyone answering the description of that unnamed second murder suspect: Morton Galloway.

After an hour of walking hot pavement and looking into cool windows Galloway's feet felt parboiled and his logical mind began to suggest that, if he kept this up, the odds were going to become increasingly against him. Not only wasn't he going to find Martinelli's name listed on a door, but that each time he stepped up and presented his face, full-view, towards one of those windows, someone out of sight inside the salons, might happen to look out and recognize in Galloway the man the police were interested in.

He finally crossed to the cooler west side of the street, entered a kosher restaurant for a glass of iced tea, and allowed his feet to cool while he watched the steady advance of evening. Finally, he was able to detect a coolness coming into the cement world, and with it, he was also able to detect in himself a strengthening suspicion that Anthony Martinelli was not a dealer, but was a dealer's muscle, and that complicated the hell out of things — unless, of course his invisible helpers, the newspaper reporters, had come up with something fresh in the late editions.

He paid for his chilled tea, left the restaurant and walked without haste towards the nearest kiosk where newspapers were sold. There, he bought two late editions, each published by a separate press, and returned to the car for the short drive back to his duplex. He drove once past, once around the block, before he put up the car and went inside. Not that he expected anything so soon, but it was not a bad idea to begin to develop a wariness; shortly now he would have to incorporate it into his everyday life.

6

Galloway Finds a Name

Galloway's second problem, aside from the first one which had to do with maintaining his freedom, loomed closer now that he had made some progress towards locating Anthony Martinelli. He knew how close the problem was when he opened the newspapers and read them, because they both identified Tony Martinelli as an individual who worked at homicide from time to time on a contract basis, which meant in simple terms that all the walking and glass-door-reading Galloway might feel up to doing, was not going to help one bit; the only person who could name the man for whom Martinelli had killed Bernard Mitreman, was Martinelli.

The second newspaper, printed on a light green paper which was novel, to say the least, had one bit of information the first newspaper had missed acquiring. The police had arrested Tony Martinelli a half hour ahead of press-time. They had him in custody.

Galloway pondered this implication. He felt reasonably sure Martinelli was not going to put his neck into anyone's noose by admitting murder, and by naming his employer as an accomplice, but Martinelli was an unknown factor, so, in Galloway's view, who had also brushed against the law a time or two from the wrong side, Martinelli's choices were pretty basic. He could exchange an admission, perhaps, for some kind of leniency, or he could leave it up to his employer to make certain Martinelli was protected. His employer in the Mitreman affair was probably in a much worse situation than Martinelli was, if one considered a successful businessman's commercial goodwill and family-life, worth anything.

The key, of course, was Martinelli's attorney. Galloway went to bed early reflecting upon this, and the following morning bright and early he drove over to the handsomely landscaped headquarters building of the Beverly Hills Police Department, read a newspaper in the shade of some benches and trees across the road and northward a short distance, and counted eleven men with briefcases who entered the building after parking their cars out front, in the area reserved for relatives and lawyers of prisoners. He had no special plan, but by eleven o'clock when he had watched those same eleven briefcases file outside again, an inkling arrived that drove him to a nearby pay-telephone in a little glass kiosk. From this place he telephoned the police station identifying himself as the special investigator for Tony Martinelli's lawyer, and asked to speak to the lawyer. The officer he spoke to, a gruff man, answered shortly. 'He was here and left about a half hour ago.'

Galloway sounded disappointed. 'Did he say where he'd be next? This is very critical.'

'Mister,' said the gruff officer, 'when Howard Bennison starts confiding in the police, I'll make application to the nearest monastery. Okay?'

Galloway said, 'Okay,' and rang off. It took him ten minutes to find the law office of Howard Bennison. It was over on La Brea Boulevard. He drove over there, had the devil's own time of it finding a place to leave the car, and was limp as a rag from the breathless, smoggy heat, by the time he got into the high-rise offices building where Bennison was listed on the lobby wall-directory as having a suite on the tenth floor. He stood in the lobby enjoying the air-conditioning for a while, then rode up to the tenth floor and killed a half-hour waiting, hoping, to get a glimpse at the lawyer. He had to give it up, finally, because too much loitering in office building corridors wasn't healthy, and went back down to the sidewalk, found another telephone kiosk complete with a directory, and in the residential section noted Bennison's home address.

It took almost a full hour to drive out to Brentwood, west of Beverly Hills, to find the lawyer's home. It was actually an estate. The rather extensive grounds were inside a Moorish style gate, and on each side of that edifice was a wrought-iron fence topped by ornamental, but definite, wrought-iron spearheads.

The house, Spanish in architecture with a delightful old-fashioned hand-made red tile roof, and a great, cool verandah out front, was long and low and very invitingly cool looking. It was also at the end of a curving long driveway that entered at one Moorish gate and left by a second one that lay several hundred feet northward, and which was nearly covered by a superb example of scarlet-blooming tropical Bougainvillaea.

Unquestionably, regardless of the statistic that the average income of U.S. solicitors was four hundred dollars monthly, or less than labourers made, this did not apply to Howard Bennison, and probably never had applied to him.

It was refreshingly cool in Brentwood, which was much closer to the sea, and which was also more elevated, than was Beverly Hills. Galloway parked round a corner and took a pleasant little stroll, being discreet enough not to pass the Bennison estate but once, and that was when he had seen a heavy car coming up towards the northernmost gate, and managed to be down there, strolling, when the heavy car turned in. One glimpse was enough. Howard Bennison was a grey, smooth-faced, lipless and narrow-eyed man, probably about Galloway's own age, but who looked older. He did not even glance out as he passed Galloway and continued on up into his estate.

A man would have to be a fool to forsake the cool peace of that low, shaded house for a return-trip to an office over on La Brea Boulevard where the heat was insufferable once a person left the air-conditioned buildings.

Galloway banked on that all the way to the La Brea Boulevard office building, and all the way up to the tenth floor. He had not anticipated finding a receptionist or a secretary, nor even a file-clerk, still at work in the Bennison suite because it was after quitting time when he got back, nor were there any of those people at work in the Bennison offices, nor in any of the other offices up and down the lighted corridor, and this facilitated breaking and entering, something Galloway accomplished very simply by springing the reception-room frosted glass door almost a full inch just by using the leverage of his own weight. Glass doors had a much greater tolerance for being warped than did solid wooden doors, and in fact the kind of door Galloway opened in the Bennison office was not designed to resist any concerted effort to open it, anyway. The doors in office buildings, especially the glass, frosted, doors of suites leased by barristers, had locks that were only tokens of privacy.

Galloway did not relock that front door any more than he had left the door to Mitreman's room locked after he got inside.

The suite of Howard Bennison was lavish and large. There was wall-to-wall carpeting in the reception room, potted orchids, and several rather nice oil landscapes. The desk and chairs were very modern and smart, and there were three telephones on the receptionist's desk.

The second room was a large, immaculate file-room, with a double row of metal filing cabinets around two walls. There were law books from the floor to the ceiling on the other two walls, except for a recessed window in the west wall. Here too, was a very large mahogany table, and chairs to match.

The third room was patently Bennison's private office. Here, Galloway went to work opening drawers and reading correspondence. It did not occur to him until he was satisfied he was not going to find anything, to switch on the telephone casette recorder. That was when he was rewarded for this day's work. Part of the first tape was a very hurried conversation between Bennison and Tony Martinelli, but the conversation only touched upon Bennison's fee for representing Martinelli, and Bennison's agreement to come as soon as Martinelli called him. This conversation, Galloway thought, had taken place prior to Martinelli's apprehension; the killer's voice sounded quick and anxious, as though he did not believe he had very much time.

The rest of that tape was between Bennison and someone named Charles

Ballenger and touched upon probating a will. The second tape was Galloway's goldmine. Martinelli identified himself on the first go-round, then said, 'Listen, lawyer, they're on their way. I just got the call from Minden. He just heard over the radio, he told me, that the cops got a drawing of me in the mail. Bennison, the only guy who could have given them a drawing of me would be Minden. No one else knew I went out there to do that. Only that louse Minden. He's going to toss me to the lions.'

A sharp, incisive voice broke in. It undoubtedly belonged to Howard Bennison. 'Hold it, Martinelli. You're not using your head. What possible reason could John Minden have for turning you in? He'd be sticking his own head into the cyanide chamber; he'd be letting you think exactly what you are thinking right now, and that would make it look to him as though you might sing to the police. Nope, I don't buy this about Minden. There's got to be someone else.'

Martinelli snorted. 'Who? I told you just like I told him, didn't no one see me.

I come in and I went out and there wasn't no one.'

Bennison was not baffled; in fact, he didn't even sound as though he cared. 'Look, Martinelli, play it cool. I'll see that you're released on bail. Just play it cool. Don't go anywhere near Minden's shop, and don't forget for one lousy minute the cops will have a tail on you. And there is one other small detail — you could drop by here and leave a deposit. I don't operate without at least half the retainer in advance. Understood?'

'Understood,' growled Martinelli, and the tape spun softly for a moment before he said, 'You better be right about Minden. I don't see how you can be, but you'd better be, because if he thinks he can double-cross me he's sure wrong as all hell.'

Bennison's voice snapped out his next words. 'I said, keep cool. Don't lead the cops anywhere but over to my office, when you're sprung. And whatever else you do, don't say a word. Not a lousy word. If I'm there, okay, otherwise, not a single damned word.'

That ended the conversation, and it gave Galloway not only a name, John Minden, but also food for thought. He could guess who John Minden was, and he was confident of locating him, but he also had to try and figure out the matter of timing: Had Bennison arranged for Martinelli's release from custody, as the conversation implied would be done, this very afternoon, and if so, had Martinelli and Bennison met in the same office where Galloway now stood? If so — and he thought it very probable — where was Martinelli right now, but perhaps more to the point from the stand-point of Galloway's personal interest, where was *John Minden* right now?

Galloway left Bennison's private office exactly as he had found it, passed out into the receptionist's room, saw the shadow fall across the frosted door out in the empty corridor, and turned on the ball of one foot to glide into the filing-room with two big strides, ease around beside the partially opened door, and hold his breath.

Someone rattled the corridor door,

then opened it. Galloway tensed, waiting for the sound of someone entering. What happened was that someone out there uttered a low grunt, punched the door-lock and closed the door, rattling it loudly to make certain it was truly locked. Galloway let his breath out slowly. He had over-looked the guards, and that was a flaw. Most American buildings of size had armed guards who made rounds on the hour, or sometimes on the half-hour. The increase in vandalism over the past decade or so had made this an almost nation-wide procedure.

Galloway timed the guard on his wristwatch, and when he felt certain the man had to be well away, Galloway went out front, opened the door, looked, found himself quite alone, and stepped out.

That was only the first step. He had to dodge guards on nine floors before reaching the street-level. Riding the lift down to the basement because he did not want to have it stop in the lobby where there would most certainly be a guard's station, kept him from perhaps meeting anyone on those intervening floors, but the moment he left the lift below street-level, he heard someone coming briskly down some metal steps, and moved swiftly to get as close as he dared to the side of that same wall.

A grey, paunchy man in a black uniform and wearing a holstered pistol hove into view craning towards the lighted lift. Galloway let him get within five feet of the last step, then reached through, tripped the guard, and hastened over his body back up the metal steps two at a time. There was no other way. Even after Galloway got out of the building and into the warm, dark street beyond, and knew he was home free, he was disgusted with himself for having had to do that.

7

The First Error

By nine o'clock that evening Galloway had zeroed in on John Minden, and ironically enough, Minden owned the Beverly Galleries, a very elegant art salon that Galloway had visited from the outside at least three times. The place was over on North Camden Drive. It was one of those larger-than-average shops that had a smoked, or dark-tinted, front window and an invitingly pleasant interior. It was also one of those business establishments where, without ever entering, one got the definite impression that no business was transacted in there that did not involve a very respectable amount of money.

Galloway looked at his watch, considered the feasibility of going out to North Camden Drive, and allowed his better sense to dissuade him because, even in broad daylight and with ample time to make a cursory examination of the premises, it was very often impossible to detect what variety of protective device these places employed. Going in cold, at night, in a neighbourhood where he did not even know the alleyways and the police-patrol routines, was a kind of rash invitation to figurative suicide. What Galloway could *not* afford, was even a questioning by the police. Not at this point in his investigation, because he was nearing the end of his undertaking, now.

Impatience got a lot of good men into trouble. Galloway told himself that over a gin-and-tonic, and went to a shaded front window, glass in hand, to gaze out over the orderly and peaceful rooftops of his neighbourhood. There were quite a few lighted residences and apartments scoring the darkness, but there were just as many places showing no lights at all. Early to bed made Jack healthy, wealthy, and wise. It also made him miss seeing things like black-and-white police cruisers making a slow patrol-run through the streets of Beverly Hills.

Galloway watched the cruiser and had a chilling kind of baseless premonition. He sighed, finished his drink and went off to bed. In the morning he was going to have to move again. By now the police were certainly looking for him, if not by name then at least by description. And he wouldn't bet they didn't have his name and his history. It was impossible to conceal those things from the police nowadays. They could back-track him from the airline to London. Maybe Inspector Merritt would cover for him, and maybe he wouldn't. It was more than possible Merritt would not even know when the request for information came in. Merritt was an Inspector, not an Identification Clerk.

Galloway slept well. Like all men with a convenient conscience, he seldom lay awake very long. Also, the prospect of moving again made him feel resigned to this one final rest in a comfortable bed. He knew that his next move was going to have to entail some of the characteristics of gypsy living. He was certain that by now, no matter where he moved in, the

Beverly Hills police could find him within two or three hours.

There was a good possibility, if Martinelli had convinced them he was the murderer, that they might not be looking very hard for Galloway. The trouble with this kind of thinking was that while he was doing it, someone could stroll up and tap him on the shoulder.

When he arose the following morning, very early, even before sun-up, he bathed, dressed, then moved all his effects down to the rented car and was gone before daybreak. He had paid for a week and had left the landlord richer by payment for four days. The landlord would never complain.

By nine o'clock Galloway had breakfasted, had parked the car down a shady side-street off North Camden Drive, and had walked back to consider the front of the Beverly Galleries, and after a while, the rear of the building from around in the alleyway, where he had to pull into someone's private parking slot to let a refuse-gathering truck go by.

In front, Minden's store was protected

by one of those invisible beams. Anyone stepping through it tripped a light in the office farther back. This kind of a protective device was neither new nor foolproof. At night, by changing the switch, the light did not come on when the beam was broken, but an alarm was rung in police headquarters. Ordinarily, and with luck, when such a beam was in place, by getting down flat and crawling forward, one could get beneath the invisible light without tripping it. At Beverly Galleries there were four wall-to-wall projectors ranging in height from four inches off the floor to chest height. They could not be stepped over nor crawled under.

Out back, the building was solid cement with no windows and one very massive steel door. It would take a half-hour and an electrical drill to bore through the lock. It would also require the making of noise, and without much doubt the door was also wired to police headquarters.

Galloway drove out of the alleyway smiling. He knew how to get into the building.

It was beginning to be a hot morning when he looked up John Minden's home address in a telephone book, and cruised over to Palm Drive to find the house. It was one of those older homes with a long history of good care. Even the grounds showed that someone manicured them at least once a week. There were several banana trees along the low, north wall, and southward, also cutting off the view and giving privacy, were thick strands of shrubbery.

Galloway also knew how to break and enter this place.

He drove back to North Camden Drive, left the car and entered a kosher restaurant across from Beverly Galleries, was fortunate to get a table near the shaded front window, and ordered pastrami on rye and a glass of iced tea. The pastrami was delicious. The tea, like all American tea, was so weak it tasted like bottled bathwater even when Galloway squeezed half a lemon into it.

No one bothered him. He had a very leisurely early lunch, and the restaurant, which was also a delicatessen, did a very brisk business, otherwise.

Shortly before he finished he saw a short, quick-moving, expensively clad man enter the store across the street, and even though the distance was great and the man's face was not visible for long, Galloway recognized Howard Bennison. He had to smile. After warning Martinelli not to go anywhere near Minden because the police would be waiting for him to do something like that, Bennison had done it, as though he did not believe the police would tail Martinelli to his attorney, then neglect to also put a tail on Bennison.

Galloway arose, paid, and strolled outside to look up and down the busy street for the tail. There were half a dozen idlers who could have been Bennison's shadow. Galloway lit a cigarette and waited until Bennison left Beverly Galleries, then saw two of the idlers turn and very casually follow Bennison back to where he had parked that tank-like big cream-coloured Cadillac.

Galloway finished his smoke and shook his head. In a land where criminals and their shady associates relied so much on guns, there seemed to be a definite inability, or at least a definite unwillingness, to use brains.

Galloway shrugged, decided he now had to decide on which course of action to pursue, and strolled back to the parked car. It was a little past high noon when he got in and sat a thoughtful moment behind the steering wheel, then drove back to the Minden house for the worst possible kind of a breaking-and-entering: The broad daylight kind.

Gaining access was no trouble. He approached the front door, rang the bell, organized his thoughts and had the spiel ready — he was selling insurance — and had to ring the bell again, until finally, with rising hopes, he deduced that either Minden's wife or housekeeper was out marketing, or he had neither and lived alone, and went to work to open the door from the outside. And failed. This time he was up against a solid wooden panel, perhaps three to four inches thick. It could not be warped and he had no picking tools. The alternative, then, was to find an unlocked window. That, of course, might expose him to watchful neighbours, but he minimized that by staying to the front and north side of the house where those ugly old banana trees helped conceal him. The bathroom window was open. He had little difficulty removing the screen and gaining access, then he got a surprise: A stereo set was playing, the music, muted though it was, and resonant with drums and brass, did not seem loud enough to have drowned out the doorbell, but most important of all, someone was undoubtedly listening.

Galloway sighed, loosened his jacket, stepped out of the bathroom, moved over carpeted floors towards a study off the rather old-fashioned and elegant dining-room, where the music was coming from, and got almost to the doorway leading into the study when he heard the music suddenly stop. He glided hastily forward and sideways to flatten beside the study doorway, reach inside for his revolver, and wait for whoever was in the study to come out. No one did, but Galloway got the answer as to why the person in the study had not heard the doorbell. Someone in there dropped a headset of padded earphones on a couch where Galloway could hear them emitting sounds. The person who had taken them off his head was evidently putting in a fresh tape.

Galloway took a chance, leaned as far as he dared, and looked around the doorjam. The man was facing him, head down while he worked with the stereo. He was not exceptionally tall, and he was built rather like Bernard Mitreman had been built.

Galloway drew slowly back and leaned upon the wall waiting for the man to pick up his earphones and get comfortable again.

Tony Martinelli!

Galloway, whose original intention had been to ransack any private drawers he could find in order to get some kind of lead on John Minden, decided now that he had all the information he needed for the time being, and slipped back across the house to the bathroom, heard the muted music commence again, stepped from the johnny-seat to the window and dropped to the spongy grass outside, and put the screen back into place. As he walked briskly back where he had left the car he wondered why Martinelli had so deliberately disobeyed Howard Bennison. He made a very bad mistake then, too. He completely overlooked the very thing Bennison had warned Martinelli about. Even when he heard the heavy footfalls behind him as he came closer to the parked car, he did not associate them with the trap he had blundered into until they came closer, picking up speed, then he knew, in one chilling moment, what a dumb thing he had done.

He had time enough to comfort himself with the thought that everyone does something stupid once in a while. Of course, with most people, the consequences are simple embarrassment. With Galloway in the present circumstances, it was not going to be simple chagrin. He loosened his jacket again, slowed a little as he approached the parked car, and strolled right on past it. Then the detective spoke and Galloway coiled like a spring.

'Hold it, mister. Police.'

Galloway halted, did not face around, and when the officer stopped about fifteen feet back, well out of Galloway's reach, there was really only one thing to do. Galloway did it. He turned slowly as he spoke. 'What do you want with me? I sell insurance and . . . ' He tipped up the reinforced three inch gunbarrel. 'Take it out very carefully, please, and throw it over into the flowers on your left.'

The detective was studying Galloway's face very intently. He did precisely as Galloway ordered, but there was no hint of fear at all as the detective said, 'Look, mister, you're not in serious trouble — yet. But you sure as hell will be now, if you do this.'

Galloway said, 'Throw it,' and the officer obeyed, but he was still not the least bit troubled.

'You are the other one,' he told Galloway. 'I know from your accent. Just explain one thing to me, Englishman: What the hell is your stake in this mess?'

Galloway smiled. 'Turn around and walk back the way you came. Don't stop and don't look back.'

For a moment the big, husky detective considered Galloway and his weapon, and shook his head at both. 'You're only botching things up,' he complained, but he turned and started walking.

Galloway did not think the detective would do anything ridiculous. American policemen did not, as a general rule, argue with people holding guns. Galloway went over to the car, got in, started the motor with the gun on the seat beside him, whipped the vehicle around in the middle of the street, an infraction of California traffic laws, but hardly to be considered at this point, and went hastening back down towards the main area of Beverly Hills.

He of course would have been discovered, inevitably, but it galled him very much to have it happen this way; in a manner he should have anticipated, and like a fool hadn't thought about.

The car, of course, was no longer of any use to him either. That disarmed detective back there would have memorized the licence number.

Galloway swore and headed into the

busiest section of Beverly Hills to lose himself. He had never for a moment thought he was going to be successful without some kind of physical contact with the opposition, either the police or John Minden, Mitreman's American contact, but he had had some idea it would not occur until he was farther along with his strategy.

8

The Art Student

Getting rid of the car posed no problem. He simply drove it back to the parking lot of the people from whom he had rented it, left enough money to cover the use of it on the seat along with the keys, then he took a taxi back to the third-rate rooming-house where he had taken a room on the second floor overlooking the front street.

This was not an ideal situation, but that blunder at the Minden house hadn't really left him much in the way of alternatives. And he decided now that with very little time left, he was going to have to hasten his operations.

He had to make a physical contact of his own, finally. Originally, he had been worried about finding Mitreman's murderer. Now, knowing who that was, he was able to bypass the killer because he knew who had sent Martinelli to visit Mitreman, and *that* was the physical contact Galloway now had to make.

The hell of it was that yesterday, or even earlier in the morning of the same day he'd had his encounter with the detective, he could have simply walked in and rammed a gun into Minden's ribs and taken him for a walk. Now, the police knew Galloway was interested in Minden. Interested enough to break into Minden's house, and that would make the police especially curious and watchful.

He knew how to get into the dealer's salon. He also knew the police would be watching John Minden now, in their effort to apprehend the second — the very elusive and mysterious — Englishman. They may, or they may not, have suspected that Minden had sent Martinelli to hit Bernard Mitreman. In Galloway's opinion they would have to be especially dense not to have arrived at some such suspicion, because by now they knew Mitreman was also an art dealer, in a most unorthodox manner. They might also have something on

Minden. If he was a criminal accomplice of Mitreman's, then he probably had not become one overnight, and would have a police record.

Whether the American authorities got a conviction against Minden, or even Martinelli, for Mitreman's murder, did not actually interest Galloway very much at the moment. Minden knew where the stolen art work was. Galloway wanted it quite badly, and that was about the size of it. Martinelli was about as important now to Galloway as were the Beverly Hills police, with the difference being that while he was reasonably certain he could avoid meeting Martinelli, he was not equally as certain of avoiding the police.

It was John Minden's reaction that interested him most. Did Minden suspect, or realize, that he was under police surveillance; did he have any idea that Martinelli had led the police to him; and how was it that Martinelli was in Minden's house, unless Minden himself had either sent him over there, or had at least agreed to Martinelli being there?

Martinelli had to be a fool to have done

what he did, particularly after being warned against doing anything like it by his attorney. Or — was this Martinelli's way of getting back at the man he thought had given the police that drawing of Martinelli?

Galloway lit a cigarette, went down the hall to shower, to wash away the greasy feeling that invariably accompanied the smog, and when he got dressed afterwards in a loose-fitting pair of slacks, with a polo-shirt beneath a light jacket, he made himself a gin-and-tonic in the dingy little room while he speculated on what he would need for what he planned to do this evening, after night-fall. The gun, of course, and a packet of cookies from his supply of groceries, otherwise just a good bit of luck, and steel nerves. It was one thing to break-and-enter, and it was something else to enter-and-not-depart.

It was an exceptionally long day, not entirely because Galloway had to kill time waiting for it to end, but also because as springtime advanced the sun stayed up-there longer.

Galloway went out for a newspaper,

and that allowed him to use up an hour reading. The Mitreman murder was now to be found on the second page, and in a routine, short column. It had obviously lost its appeal as a sensational bit of local news. In the article Galloway read, it said the suspect, Martinelli, had won release on bond. It also said that the murdered man was rumoured to have been a shady character overseas and there was even a speculation that perhaps someone had followed him from England to either shoot him, or to hire him shot.

Galloway grimaced. That was an oblique accusation that, he, the mysterious second Englishman, might have followed Mitreman. It gave him an insight into one kind of police thinking. Probably, after his run-in with the detective earlier, it was decided that, since the second Englishman had a gun, he just might have been after Mitreman too.

If the police kept working on this theory, they were not going to view Minden as much of a suspect. Galloway lit a cigarette, blew smoke, and decided that this really was not likely to involve him. What he had to do was visit Minden, and he had to do it with more finesse than he had demonstrated today when he'd visited Minden's residence. This time there could be no police.

Finally, when the lessening noise told Galloway it was either quitting time in the commercial district, or early dinner-time, he went outside to test the dusk and found it a little bright yet, but with a brisk walk ahead of him before he got up to North Camden Drive, he struck out.

He thought of Inspector Merritt, and inevitably thought of Merritt's melodramatic suggestion of the beard and dyed hair. It wasn't corny any longer.

He also wondered if Merritt had his letter yet. Normally, air mail letters reached London in four or five days. If Merritt had the letter, all he knew was that Mitreman had been murdered. That might induce a great sigh of relief, but it might also induce some concern for Galloway — except that Galloway did not think it would. Merritt had said, 'One last time', and damn his soul to hell, one more bad slip for Galloway and it just might be his last time. One man was dead and another man was a professional murderer — with Morton Galloway in between. It was difficult, knowing Inspector Merritt, not to believe he might at least have had some inkling of how this affair might turn out for Galloway.

In fact, the more Galloway dwelt upon it, the more it occurred to him that when Merritt had said, 'One last time,' damn his soul, he probably had meant it in an altogether different, and more sinister way, than Galloway had thought at the time. Merritt might just have been hoping to get rid of them *both*, Mitreman *and* Galloway.

By the time Galloway reached North Camden Drive he was limber and perspiring, which was a good thing for what lay ahead. He was also in a properly disagreeable frame of mind.

Most of the shops were closed and locked, with their nightlights on, inside, but there was still a good bit of both wheeled and pedestrian, traffic, and the fact that Galloway entered the alleyway that led to the rear of Beverly Galleries, was a matter of absolutely no interest at all, particularly since he was lost in the gloom within minutes of having gone up there.

The alleyway was totally empty. The buildings whose backs were turned to it on both sides, were as blank and uninspiring as the back of most buildings were. It was also darker in the alleyway than elsewhere, and when Galloway reached his destination and moved over into the dense gloom where the refuse tins were racked up on a waist-high stand, for easy access to the refuse trucks, even if someone had been watching, or looking accidentally, in that direction, they'd have had to have been closer than ten feet to see Galloway step up among the trash bins and stand perfectly still there.

One of the most considerate things fire and safety authorities in most cities did, was provide fire-escapes and steel wall-ladders on buildings. Galloway ran up the side of Minden's building like a lanky spider and stepped over on to the flat, tarred roof, without even marring the crease in his trousers.

The rooftop was hot to the touch although the sun had been gone for more than an hour. It was not difficult to imagine how hot that black tar was *before* sunset. It was also soft and pliable, especially over where the skylight was raised slightly, to preclude the possibility of rainwater running down inside the salon, and where Galloway ascertained that, as he had expected, the green-tinted, wire-mesh, very thick skylight-windows had been securely barred and bolted from inside.

Galloway made his appraisal, then walked over to the front edge of the roof and smoked a cigarette while he stood perfectly still in his brown attire, looking all around. There were no higher rooftops nearby, although in the distance, down towards Wilshire Boulevard, there were a lot of high-rise office buildings. Neither were there any people looking across at him, nor even glancing up from down below on the sidewalks.

He had not expected to be seen, but he *did* expect police cars to cruise through now and then. Beverly Hills was a very wealthy community, both in the residential and the commercial areas. It taxed itself stiffly to provide plenty of protection, too.

Galloway waited until he had finished his smoke. He was in no hurry, and now, of all times, he wanted to be absolutely certain he was not going to meet another detective. If it happened this time, tonight, without any question he was not going to be able to walk away again. His plan called for Galloway to place himself in a corner, something he did not especially relish, but something he believed had to be done. This was, he felt, his final act. After tonight he expected — hoped very much, anyway — to be able to fly home. It would be very nice to be in a land where the temperature in springtime did not reach one hundred and ten degrees, and where tea tasted like tea.

To get past those wire-mesh, green skylight panes of inch-thick glass Galloway took a good bit of that pliable tar around the skylight housing, pressed it flat over the centre of the nearest window until it covered an area approximately eight inches by eight inches, then he proceeded to strike the tar smartly with the barrel of his revolver, a procedure that put great stress upon the glass, but which made no noise, thanks to the muffling effect of the roofing tar. When the glass finally broke, Galloway was able to lift it out a piece at a time, put it carefully aside, and reach through until he could feel the wooden bar that was bolted below the windows. He had no tools for removing the bolt, and in fact he did not plan to remove it. It took him more than an hour to lift out all the glass from one window, and he did such a masterful job of it, using tar to prevent any glass from dropping through and crashing to the floor below, that he had some idea the police would probably respect his finesse.

Because Galloway was not a fat man, he wedged himself through the glass opening, gripped the bolted wooden bar below, which now served him admirably as he hung suspended, and when he was satisfied that the drop was no more than fifteen feet, he let go, at the same time swinging his body so that when he lit it would be where a sofa stood against a cement wall.

He landed soundlessly, bounced off the sofa, and stood perfectly still for a moment, then turned and examined the small room where he was. Evidently this place was used for Minden and his hired help when they had luncheon on the premises. There were some plates on a shelf, and there was a coffee pot standing upon a plugged-in small hotplate. Several smocks hung from pegs, and a woman's coat with a fur collar, hung from a hanger on the back of the door.

Galloway could have switched on the overhead light, there were no windows, but instead he approached the door without touching anything, leaned to make absolutely certain there was no alarm beam, then opened the door and found himself in a curtained-off short hallway where it was as dark as the inside of a closet.

Beyond the curtain was Minden's large and very elegant main display salon. Every wall was covered with excellent art work. Some of the frames were severely plain and modern and some, the majority, were very ornate and old-appearing.

This large, gloomy room was lighted by reflected street lamps outside, and by the diverted, or refracted, soft brightness of two small window-lights, one on each side of the tinted-glass display counter out front facing the street. Cruising police cars would be able to see in, but thanks to that modishly tinted glass, unless the officers stopped, got out and stood directly in front of the window, they would be unable to distinguish movement.

Galloway had plenty of time. He strolled from painting to painting giving each valuable bit of art work his undivided attention. He was no connoisseur, and in fact he wasn't even familiar with the paintings he was here to steal back, but like all earthy and mundane souls, Galloway knew what pleased him, it did not even have to be good art; some he liked and some he thought were terrible.

9

A Quiet Night

There were two storerooms, one seeming to serve as a re-framing and touching-up room as well as a storage facility. Here, going through drawers and making a rather minute and time-consuming examination, Galloway came across a small, dented metal tag that was engraved with the legend: Bedford Art Gallery, London. He pocketed that, went on with his exploring, and although he found a pile of discarded old frames, among which he felt certain would be the woodwork removed from Mitreman's flat frame, the one that held the six stolen pictures on their trip to America, he did not look for it.

In the other storeroom there were racks of paintings and more of them hanging upon all the walls. This room was evidently the place where John Minden first took his acquisitions to be perhaps cleaned up and retouched, if that were necessary, before they were taken out and hung in the main salon.

Galloway looked at several dozen paintings and found just two that appealed to him. One was of a rural scene in England — at least he *thought* it was the Midlands — with several people standing idly in the shade of a great tree near a busy little watercourse. The other painting he liked was of a bosomy woman with creamy skin, large, dark eyes, and a mouth that curved perfectly. The dress was old-fashioned, but the eyes and mouth were as fresh and inviting as yesterday. Being a bachelor had its disadvantages, even when one was illegally in an art salon at midnight on a hot springtime California night.

When Galloway found his final destination, John Minden's private office, he sat at the beautiful old antique oaken desk, brought out the packet of cookies he had brought along, got comfortable in the gloom and had his midnight snack.

Afterwards, he was very careful to

sweep away the crumbs and to put the celophane wrapper back into a pocket instead of into the copper-hammered waste-bin beside the desk.

He also smoked, swivelled around to study the paintings hanging in the elegant office, which were undoubtedly Minden's personal favourites, and decided that his rural scene and the dark-eyed girl were far better.

When he stumped out the smoke in a half-filled large glass ashtray, it was time, he told himself, to go to work.

John Minden's files were minutely kept. It was rather a vignette of the man himself to see how meticulous he was about his records. Every transaction had its separate folder, and each folder, whether it held two papers or fifteen papers, was arranged by date. Minden, whatever else he did, obviously had a fetish about being correct and orderly. It was an unusual variety of pedantry in a crook, Galloway thought, then qualified that by saying to himself that it was an unusual thing in *common* crooks, but evidently John Minden was not just a common crook. He ran a lucrative legitimate business on the side.

It seemed, according to the records Galloway took back to the desk to study, to be a fairly good legitimate business. There was a month-by-month financial summary, a kind of balance-sheet that Minden kept which would tell him at a glance how he was faring. Galloway did not find that right away, not until after he had waded through most of the files racked up alphabetically from A to D, but when he came upon it, eventually, it showed him not only that Minden's legitimate enterprise was profitable — not wildly so but certainly adequately so, providing Minden were not a greedy individual — it also showed him that Minden's smooth and very proper book-keeping system had a completely honest face to show to the world, should the world come snooping, and that of course meant that John Minden, like a lot of businessmen, kept two sets of records, one for the Internal Revenue snoops, the other for his own private edification. It was the second set of records Galloway needed. He was satisfied, after an hour or so of looking at the legitimate records, that John Minden was a very sophisticated and worldly — crook.

But the files showed nothing but what Galloway had already discovered; showed nothing but Minden's prim and proper accounting. Even his bookkeeping system, as nearly as Galloway could make out, jibed perfectly with his business summary and his records of sales and purchases as shown by the manila folders.

Minden had to spend a good bit of time here in his office juggling records to have such an ideal set of records. Galloway began forming a picture of a calm, very capable, highly knowledgeable individual, with ice-water for blood. If the police had never mauled John Minden it was probably because they had no inkling about his real crookedness.

Galloway had to break a letter-opener to get the top desk drawer prised open, and he had to break the drawer's little lock to accomplish that. He had reason. The files were a beautiful job of camouflage.

Any accountant or book-keeper brought in by the police or even the income tax people, would never be able to find anything wrong with those files, but somewhere Minden had his own accounting system.

If it was in his head, which was probable, there still had to be external records. Nowadays, there was no way under the sun to have a completely anonymous accounting system. Galloway proved it, finally, after he had pawed through the neat, numerically-arranged bank envelopes in a lower desk drawer. The bank statement for this very month showed that although the cheque had not been sent in for deposit, which meant that Minden had presented it to be cashed personally, and had then taken the cash away with him, the bank recorded on his statement for the month that there had been a cheque paid out in the amount of two hundred and twenty-five thousand dollars.

Galloway sat down and studied that entry very carefully. He checked it against the monthly balance to be sure the money had not been deposited, then he went back to the summary-file and found nothing at all about that entry in those listings. Minden had obviously taken the quarter of a million dollars in cash and since the cheque, like the withdrawal, were the same day, and that date coincided with the second day after Bernard Mitreman arrived in the States, it did not seem too improbable that the quarter of a million was money Minden got from some art collector for the stolen Mitreman-paintings.

The hell of it was, that bank statements listed only dates and amounts, not the names of people who made out cheques.

Galloway put the pieces together. Minden knew what art work Mitreman was bringing. He may even have had a hand in telling Mitreman which art work to steal, but that was neither here nor there at the moment. What mattered was that Mitreman and Minden had a beautiful arrangement: Mitreman arrived in the country, flew directly to Beverly Hills, handed over the stolen paintings, and Minden had them sold within two days for cash. Minden *may* have just been lucky, but more likely someone he knew had already agreed to purchase the paintings. Perhaps the purchaser was also involved in the dishonest aspects of the affair, although that was simply a wild guess on Galloway's part as he sat studying the bank statement.

The rest of it was fairly easy to figure out. Minden, with a quarter of a million dollars, which was one hell of a lot of cash, was obliged to pay Mitreman a healthy share, perhaps a hundred thousand or maybe a full one-half. It was much less expensive to hire someone to hit Mitreman. It was possible to hire murder done in America on a sliding scale; some killers worked for as little as one thousand dollars per murder, but Galloway's guess was that a man with Martinelli's reputation probably worked for five or ten thousand, and that left Minden with all the rest of that quarter of a million dollars for himself. Thousands of people were knocked off every year for a fraction as much.

Galloway slowly put away the records, being particularly careful to replace them exactly as he had found them, with the exception of that most recent bank statement listing the cashed quarter of a million cheque. He had an idea how that revealing piece of paper was going to serve him as a classical red herring.

It was three-thirty in the morning by the time he had everything tidied up again. His long wait would be over before too many more hours ran past.

He went back to the small room where the hotplate was and made himself a pot of coffee. Of the five crockery cups with initials painted on them in red enamel paint, he chose the one with the letter O on it, because that amused him; the letter O could of course refer to a name, but it might also signify that this cup was reserved for guests. Galloway most certainly was a guest. A unique one, an uninvited and even an unknown one, but still a guest.

The coffee was fresh-tasting, which was a surprise. It brightened Galloway's perspective a little. He took the cup marked O and returned to the office puzzling over the identity of that art-lover who had paid Minden a quarter of a million dollars. Galloway had hoped he might find Mitreman's stolen art work in Minden's salon, but he had seriously doubted that was going to obtain after going over the storerooms, and also after discovering the dented Bedford Gallery brass tag.

It certainly would have simplified the hell out of things if he could have located the stolen paintings, because by four in the morning he could have been back at his rooming-house packing.

He hadn't really been that optimistic, though. People who dealt, not just in stolen art work but also in murder, did not leave incriminating evidence around for just anyone to stumble over, and John Minden, of all people, was patently a notch above average in just about any way a person chose to assess him.

There was no record of who had paid that quarter of a million dollars, although Galloway found a list of people who apparently were Minden's customers. The list did not say exactly who all those people were, but it seemed fairly obvious.

There was a figure in dollars and cents beside each name, too, as though Minden had either sold these people art work for that amount, or as though he had them evaluated as being able to spend that much.

The trouble with this list was that Galloway was convinced it was not complete. There were, for example, about fifty more files in the cabinets listing individual transactions by the name of the purchasers, then there were names on the un-titled list.

For all Galloway could figure out that list might have been for people who would buy, and not who had already bought. Minden, the careful and expert record-keeper, would not be above keeping that kind of a list too.

Galloway made a copy all the same, even though there was no name on that list that showed someone who might have paid, or who might be willing to pay, a quarter of a million dollars for art work. Galloway simply had the time to kill, and this was not a bad way to kill it.

He finished his coffee at five o'clock,

took the cup back and placed it exactly where he had found it, sauntered one more time through the storerooms and through the main salon, then stood a moment looking out through the smoked front window for some sign of paleness in the eastern sky. It was out there, a kind of watery, diluted shade of weak blue.

Galloway rubbed his chin, felt the stubble, smiled to himself and returned to the office to take out the revolver and examine it. Odd thing about people, but handguns always seemed to make their normal resolve crumple without them ever questioning the fact that a man holding a gun was very seldom motivated in a manner that would encourage him to shoot. The answer to that, of course, was that people simply chose not to run any risks because guns at close range were very final, and what they caused when fired at close range, was even more final.

Galloway had not fired a gun since his army days. He hadn't liked doing it then and the idea of doing it now was so alien to his psychology that he could smile to himself, *about* himself; anyone who knew Morton Galloway would have smiled too, at the prospect of him deliberately firing a gun at anyone.

Of course, where Galloway was now, no one knew him that well. In fact, except for the prying police, probably no one knew him at all, not even his name, and that was what he was relying on as he glanced at his watch when seven o'clock rolled around, to make his present incursion a success.

He had time for one last smoke, and he enjoyed it while watching the slow hands of his watch creep round towards eight in the morning. It had been a long night but not an especially boring one. He had rather thought it might not prove boring.

He knew some things he had only suspected before, and he also had some questions now that he hadn't had the evening before. At eight-thirty he heard someone rattling the front, streetside door, and thought he was finally on the verge of finding a lot of answers.

10

A Cheque and One Man's Name

More than one person entered, because Galloway heard voices out in the main salon. He thought they were all women until he heard a man's lower, crisper tones, and that was a relief. If he had spent that whole long night waiting in vain, it would have been more than just a bitter disappointment.

Someone just outside Minden's private office started a technical conversation. Galloway listened with interest while the man's crisp voice gave both an explanation and instructions, then Galloway heard the woman walking away, and the office door swung inward. Galloway did not move until the door closed and the lean, rather tense-looking conservatively attired greying man stepped towards the oaken desk. Galloway slid behind him and barred the door.

The newcomer almost sat down behind the desk, then saw something, scratches around the broken lock of the uppermost drawer, and froze in a slightly bent posture while he stared. He did not raise even his eyes until some sixth sense gave the alarm, then his head moved a little, his gaze jumped to the barred door and moved up just as far as the cocked revolver, hesitated for several seconds, then moved on up to Galloway's face and stayed there.

Galloway said, 'Sit. Just keep both hands atop the desk, if you don't mind.'

It took John Minden several seconds to recover from the shock. No matter how assured and confident a man was, the stunning emergence of an armed enemy where no such thing had ever even remotely been expected, had to be traumatic.

Galloway gestured. 'Sit down.'

Minden obeyed, finally, and set both hands palms down upon his desk. 'Who are you?' he asked quietly, without a trace of tremor in his voice. 'What are you doing in here?'

The answer to the first question was not forthcoming, and the answer to the second question was obvious: Galloway was in there, and had waited in there all night, to avoid the police. Not the police that might recognize him, but the police he was sure were now following John Minden.

Galloway had to recover some paintings without being intruded upon. The surest way to botch things now would be to be discovered by the police. They might be satisfied for the time being to trail someone like Minden, but they most certainly would *not* be satisfied to do this with Morton Galloway.

'I need just one answer to a riddle from you,' said Galloway. 'If you are co-operative there should be no reason why I won't leave you unharmed. It's up to you.'

Minden's eyes narrowed slightly. 'You're English.'

Galloway smiled thinly. 'Quite, but I'm a little harder to put down than Bernard Mitreman was.'

Minden's narrowed eyes grew deathly

still. 'What is this all about?'

Galloway kept smiling. 'Do we have the time for this? I could tell you, for example, that whether you knew it or not, Anthony Martinelli was listening to your stereo yesterday in the study of your residence, wearing earphones, and the police were outside to keep watch on him. And that, Mister Minden, led the police to you, through Martinelli. They will now also be keeping you under surveillance.'

Minden's hands on the desk curled into loose fists. 'I don't know anyone named Martinelli.'

Galloway shrugged. 'That's what I mean by asking if we had the time to play footsie. I'm not the police. You don't have to deny nor justify a single damned thing to me. All I'm here for is a name and I'll get it if I have to extract it from you a letter — and a bullet — at a time. But since we are both in somewhat the same unpleasant fix, I thought I'd also tell you a few facts of life. For example, the night Martinelli killed Mitreman he was seen leaving Mitreman's flat, and the person who saw him, drew a caricature and sent it to the police.'

Minden said, 'You! By God now I know who you are! Tony remembered a guy in the corridor the night of Mitreman's — accident, but until he remembered you, he thought I was trying some kind of double-cross when the police nailed him.' Minden's blue eyes turned to blue ice. 'The police know of a second Englishman. It's been in the newspapers. I didn't believe it.'

Galloway said, 'But now you do. And you had better also believe what I just told you about the cops tying Martinelli to you, after he was seen to enter your residence. If you told him to go in there, you ought to have your ruddy skull examined. Of course they'd be shagging him the moment Bennison got him released on bail. You are a novice, I take it.'

Minden glared. 'A novice! Englishman, that damned silly moron of a Martinelli was in my house yesterday without my permission, and despite what his attorney told him. He still thought I'd double-crossed him and didn't care whether he implicated me or not.'

Galloway said, 'Okay; I'll buy that, Mister Minden. And now that I've done you a favour, I want one in exchange.'

'Or,' said Minden, dropping his eyes to the gun sourly, but fearlessly, 'you'll fire. Englishman, that noise would seal you off in here without a prayer of escaping.'

Galloway knew the answer to that. 'Mister Minden, if you are right or wrong, you won't be around to find out, will you?' He tipped up the reinforced, ugly little three inch barrel. 'Who paid you that two hundred and twenty-five thousand dollars?'

Minden smiled. 'Go to hell, Limey.'

Galloway smiled right back. 'All right, but not alone. Once more, what was his name?'

'I don't know what you're talking about!'

'Look in the bank statement for this month, Mister Minden, and note where you cashed a cheque for that amount, but did not deposit the money.'

Minden's colour faded a little but his glowering stare at Galloway did not waver. 'You've been busy in here, last night, haven't you?'

'And I've made copies,' said Galloway. 'Look; you are quite right about my not shooting you. The idea doesn't appeal to me very much, which is not to say I *won't* do it, only that I'd rather not. But we don't have to deal in violence, do we? We're not Martinelli's type are we? For example, I can mail the copy I made of that bank statement to the police and they can verify its authenticity through the bank, can't they? Then they will want you to answer the same questions: Who gave you the cheque, and what did you do with the money?'

Minden leaned back in his desk-chair. 'And I'll tell them the same thing I'm telling you, Englishman: Go to hell. But I'll also refer them to my attorney.'

Galloway considered, then pushed off the door and strode calmly to face Minden from across the width of the oaken desk. He shifted the revolver to his left hand and with the speed of a light-flash, struck Minden in the face. Both the man and his chair went over backwards. When Minden struggled around from under the chair and looked up, blinking, Galloway had moved round to the same side of the desk and had put up the revolver. He said, 'I didn't say I had any aversion to a hand-to-hand discussion, Mister Minden. Only an aversion to shooting people.' He extended his left hand. 'Get up, please.'

Minden ignored the hand and scrambled back to his feet. He smoothed out his jacket and trousers, then put a palm to the reddening side of his face. There was plain murder in his blue-ice stare, but Galloway ignored that.

'Listen, Mister Minden, if you'll be reasonable and think a bit you'll discover that I'm actually befriending you. So far, you did not know the police were watching you. You did not know Martinelli had led them to you, and because Martinelli is suspected of murder, it can only be a matter of time before the police — if they haven't already done so — decided you are the one who hired Martinelli to hit Mitreman. As an accessory to murder, Mister Minden, when they arrest you, there won't be much chance to escape, will there? You can make an airline reservation this very morning and be half-way to Algeria before the Beverly Hills police even know you're running. In other words, Mister Minden, I'm giving you your only chance, and in exchange all I'm asking is a man's name: Who gave you that cheque?'

Minden stopped, set his chair upright again and dropped into it. He manipulated his jaw, seemed to find everything still in working order, and looked at Galloway with a fresh and grudging respect.

'They can't tie me to Mitreman,' he said.

Galloway shrugged that off. 'They don't have to. All they have to do is tie you to Martinelli, the man who murdered Mitreman. And from what I've deduced about Martinelli, he is one of those moronic types, who, when they force his back to a wall, will unbosom himself in exchange for some kind of deal. *You* are the only excuse for any unbosoming. Think about it.'

Minden was not ready to yield. 'He can sing his head off, it'll be his word against mine.'

Galloway very slowly shook his head from side to side, and put a sardonic gaze upon the seated man. 'Wrong again, Mister Minden. It will be your word against his — *and my word*. I can supply the police with the motive for Mitreman's murder — you had no intention of sharing any of that two hundred and twenty-five thousand with Mitreman, so you hired Martinelli to kill Mitreman. To prove it, they can verify that you were paid that money. And to go further, if they really want to dig for additional motive, I can also supply that — if necessary in exchange for amnesty and a free flight out of the country — the six paintings Mitreman had stolen in London. Mister Minden, you of all people ought to know that while two hundred and twenty-five thousand dollars in cash is anonymous, six catalogued and renowned oil paintings by moderately well-known old masters, are anything *but* anonymous. The police can find them, and tie it all together.'

Minden fished out a packet of cigarettes, lit one, then, perhaps as an afterthought, or perhaps as a peace offering, held out the pack to Galloway. But he refused and lit up from his own packet. They smiled at one another like a pair of wolves standing stiff-legged, hackles up, across the fat carcass of a freshly slain rabbit.

Minden smoked a moment, then relaxed a little. Evidently his reddening right cheek was not very painful because he ignored it. Or perhaps it *was* painful but Minden, facing something that just might be the most truly painful episode of his entire life, was not mindful of a little facial discomfort.

'What is your objective?' he asked Galloway. 'If you think you're going to get any of that money, forget it.'

Galloway neither looked nor acted especially downcast. 'Who bought the pictures?'

'Why are you so insistent about knowing that?'

'Because I want them back.'

Minden blinked. 'You plan to steal them back?'

Galloway nodded, and for a moment John Minden just stared, then he threw back his head and laughed as though this were a source of genuine amusement to him. When the laughter died and he rocked forward again, he blew smoke at Galloway, his eyes still alive with ironic merriment.

'And after I tell you, Englishman, you aren't just going to walk out of here and leave me alone, are you?'

'No. You are going after them with me.'

Minden's humour died. 'Like hell I am. I'm out of it the minute I tell you who has them.'

Galloway crossed both arms across his chest and considered the other man's narrow, long face for a moment before speaking. Minden was beginning to act more like a co-conspirator than an enemy. He obviously was eventually going to tell Galloway who had paid him all that money for those six pictures. Galloway was well over the hump; now, he was on the downhill slide towards home and safety. He could afford to be a little easy, to smile a little. Instead he unfolded his arms and looked stonily at his prisoner.

'Mister Minden, it's been a long night. I'm a little tired. I can leave you so unconscious you won't be able to remember your own name for eight hours. It's entirely up to you.'

'They send you to the gas chamber in this country for abduction,' snarled the art dealer.

Galloway was unimpressed. 'I think it's far more possible that you'll hire me killed if I *don't* keep you with me. After all, Mitreman was your *friend*, and look at what you did to him.' Galloway leaned, caught hold of Minden's jacket and hauled the other man straight up in the swivel-chair. 'I want the man's name who bought those six paintings, Mister Minden, and this is absolutely the last time I'm going to ask you.'

They looked steadily at one another from a distance of less than two feet for several stiff moments, then Galloway slowly pushed Minden back in his chair, released him, and dropped his right hand into the righthand pocket of his jacket where the snub-nosed revolver nestled.

John Minden said, 'Howard Bennison.'

For five seconds Galloway stood staring. Then he remembered something that should have rung a bell: Those delightful oil paintings in Bennison's outer office, which indicated to anyone observant enough to be aware of it, that the lawyer was an art buff. Galloway told himself gravely that he had made *two* mistakes, thus far, then he sighed and said, 'On your feet,' to John Minden, 'and out that door, through the salon to the street, and make it as natural as possible because I'll be right behind you.'

11

The Size of a Racketeer

There was no other way, unless Galloway had chosen to sit in the office until evening with Minden, and then try to elude the police.

No one glanced twice at Minden and Galloway out in the main salon except for a pert little redheaded salesgirl with tawny-tan eyes and a tipped-up nose, who turned very slowly and measured Galloway up and down. He smiled and nodded his thanks for her obvious interest, then followed Minden outside and told him to lead off in the direction of his car. Minden obeyed, but he also swung his head, looking left and right.

'Where are the police?' he asked, sounding sceptical.

Galloway did not bother to look, nor to answer. He considered the bronze-coloured Cadillac and shook his head.

Only an extraordinary crook would be seen in a car like that. Minden qualified. As he slid under the wheel and as Galloway slid in beside him, Minden twisted hard around peering out the rear window. In a mildly explosive way he said, 'By God, you're right,' faced fully forward and with both hands on the steering-wheel sat rigidly until Galloway nudged him.

'Start the car, what the hell's wrong with you, Minden? A surveillance team isn't the end of the world.'

Minden looked at Galloway, then obeyed. As soon as the Cadillac was turned out of its parking place Minden, evidently unable to resist, craned around for another look at the pair of men in the shiny, unmarked vehicle farther back.

Galloway was disgusted and gouged Minden, hard. 'Just drive, and stop acting like a schoolboy who's just spied the truant officer.'

Minden obeyed. 'Drive where?'

'Just drive,' repeated Galloway, and after they had progressed a mile or so through traffic, and grey, hot sunlighted smog, he said, 'Minden: Where can we get another car?'

The art dealer, over his first shock, was evidently thinking more clearly, finally, which was how Galloway had hoped things might turn out. Minden blew out a big breath and screwed up his face. 'One of the girls who works for me left her car at a service station not far from the gallery.'

Galloway smiled. 'Can we get back to that car, ditch this one, and do it all without the police being able to keep us in sight?'

Minden drove as far as the next intersection, then signalled to turn right and eased around with the westering traffic. 'I think so,' he muttered. 'I'm not accustomed to anything like this.'

'You'd better develop the knack,' exclaimed Galloway, leaning to study the rearward cars as they also came around the corner at that intersection back there, from an outside rearview mirror, 'because from the moment we walked out of your gallery we both became targets. If they grab you, believe me, you're a dead pigeon. What Martinelli won't pin on you in exchange for leniency, I'll tell them. Incidentally, those enterprising policemen just turned the corner back there.'

Minden romped down hard on his accelerator and the big car roared ahead. Galloway was annoyed. 'You damned idiot, let up!'

Minden obeyed, and for several squares he drove conservatively, then, with one eye on the rearview mirror, the other eye on the approaching fresh intersection, he got ready to make another turn, and Galloway, who did not know the neighbourhood very well, had to rely upon his intuitive feeling for directions. They were now heading back towards the gallery on North Camden Drive, and that meant Minden was going to drive back up where his employee had left her car.

Minden seemed to finally accept Galloway as a sort of hostile ally, as an enemy upon whom Minden had no choice but to rely. As they drove back towards the service station he even demonstrated a slight willingness to more than just accept Galloway, because he said, 'I have no experience in this sort of thing. I'm not even sure we're acting the way we should. As for the law, it can't ordinarily do anything providing you have a decent attorney.'

Galloway was not interested. 'Just get us close to where the woman left her car. As for your philosophizing, keep it for some nice evening before the fire.'

Minden shot Galloway a look. 'I don't even know your name.'

Galloway was tempted to laugh. 'Frightful breach of etiquette,' he conceded. 'We actually shouldn't be sharing the same car since we've never been properly introduced.'

Minden saw no humour in this and slowed as he pointed ahead where a car service centre stood. 'The blue car, the sporty one,' he said, 'parked over near the fence.'

Galloway had to make some rapid decisions. 'Park out front of that restaurant between here and the service centre.' As Minden slowed to obey, Galloway leaned for another look in the rearview mirror. The unmarked police car with its brace of solemn-faced passengers was a hundred yards back. Galloway had rather hoped there would be only that one parking place, because then the police would have to drive past while Minden and Galloway entered the restaurant, but Fate did not always aid those most deserving of aid. There were several additional empty places at the rearward kerbing, and as Minden's Cadillac slowed with an obvious intention of filling a parking place, the unmarked police car did the same, but farther back.

Galloway rapped out orders. 'Park it fast, cut the engine and get out quickly. Follow me into the restaurant. *Move!*'

Of course John Minden could have done just the opposite, but he didn't, and as Galloway hit the pavement and started briskly towards the restaurant, Minden came hastening from the far side of the car to join him.

Inside, the restaurant was about half full. Galloway looked for the sign indicating the direction of the rest rooms as he made his way down the central aisle, found the sign, and did not even hesitate as he went past a beefy man at

the cash register who looked up enquiringly, then who turned and watched
Galloway and John Minden disappear
beyond the swinging door leading to the
rest rooms.

Galloway locked the door after Minden,
jumped on to the toilet-seat, heaved a
strong shoulder against the closed window,
got it open, and vaulted out to land in a
cool, none-too-immaculate alleyway. Minden,
once he understood what he had to do,
managed a very creditable escape too.

They ran half-way the length of the
alleyway, slowed to a decorous walk
where the alleyway debauched upon a
busy thoroughfare, and dead ahead across
the intersection was the blue sport car.
Galloway led off and Minden came up
abreast of him as they reached the
entrance to the service station. 'If they see
us drive the car off they're probably going
to call the police because it will look as
though we are stealing the car.'

Galloway swung his head and nodded.
'Good thinking. Now shut up, slide under
the wheel and let's get out of here.'

Minden obeyed. Because the car was

due to be looked after shortly it still had the key in the ignition switch. Minden gunned the motor to life, squinted towards the glassed-in enclosure of the station where several men were at work, eased out the clutch and drove away. Galloway held his breath until they were on the asphalt apron leading out into the traffic, and after that he did not particularly care whether they were seen taking the car or not.

'Right,' he said to John Minden. 'Right up the street away from the damned café back there.' While Minden obeyed, Galloway twisted to look back and see if there was any sign of the pair of policemen ducking forth from the alleyway. There wasn't, but all that meant was that he and Minden had gained perhaps a half hour, perhaps a full hour, of freedom, then the description of the blue sport car and its licence number would be coming over the air to all police cruisers.

Minden relaxed after a mile or so of driving and looked at Galloway from a perspiring face. 'Now where to?'

'That's a silly question,' replied Galloway. 'To where the paintings are, naturally.'

Minden drove a while, then said, 'Look; I ought to let you do this because it will certainly end up with your being taken, but as long as I'm with you, that could also work against me.'

'Taken how?' asked Galloway.

'The paintings are at Bennison's residence over in Brentwood, and it is a veritable fortress. It's been his boast for years that his residence cannot be burglarized. I suppose it has something to do with the fact that Bennison has grown rich from defending criminals, that he has no faith in people at all.'

Galloway looked at Minden, his enforced ally. 'But there is a way in, isn't there?'

Minden was slow to answer that. 'I can only say that Bennison has said for years no one can break into his residence.'

Galloway, struck with a fresh idea, asked if Howard Bennison had bought other stolen works of art. Minden was bland about that.

'If you mean, do I specialize in stolen

paintings, the answer is no, I do not. But if someone like Mitreman comes to me with some works of art for sale, how am I to know they have been stolen?'

Galloway was ironic. 'Sure; of course. You are an innocent, put upon individual art dealer. Mister Minden, frankly I couldn't care less about your dealings, and you didn't answer my question, did you?'

Minden, for the first time since early morning, seemed to be almost master of the situation. He said, 'I think Mister Bennison is a real swinger. I think he not only buys stolen art, but that he buys other things, such as stolen jewellery. He does have the perfect set-up for it — defence attorney for criminals, and one of the best in the business.'

Galloway had his answer, and a glimmer more, but he still needed to know how to get inside where those six paintings were. 'You've been inside Bennison's residence, I take it.'

Minden nodded. 'I have. If you think you can wave that gun around and walk in, take my word for it, you can't. You

140

might get inside, Englishman, but you'd never get out again. At least not under your own propulsion, and standing upright.'

Galloway was annoyed by Minden's smug expression. 'But *you* are going to take me in there, without any gun-waving.'

Minden looked around. 'There's only one way. You've got to have Bennison beside you.'

Galloway smiled. 'Fine. Then we'll stop up ahead somewhere and you can telephone him to meet us at his residence. He must have faith in you. No one hands over two hundred and twenty-five thousand dollars unless they have faith in the recipient, do they?'

Minden slowed the car. 'I can't just call him and say I want to show someone his collection of art.'

'Of course you can't, Mister Minden. But you could call him and say you have several more very valuable works of art from London that he can buy at a fraction of their worth. That's how you hooked him on the works of art Mitreman brought over, isn't it?'

John Minden swallowed hard. 'And when he sees you, and when he discovers that I have no paintings with me, then what?'

'We'll use the gun if necessary,' replied Galloway, but Minden began shaking his head very emphatically before that had all been said.

'I've been trying to tell you,' exclaimed Minden, 'that his house is a fortress. That gun isn't going to do anything but get you killed. I don't mind that, except that I'll be with you.'

Galloway began to form an opinion of the attorney Howard Bennison, and it had to do with a lot more than simply six stolen oil paintings from London, and one murdered dealer in illicit art. He motioned for Minden to pull over to the kerbing. They were just entering the environs of the outlying and exclusive area where Howard Bennison lived. There was practically no traffic. In fact, they could actually hear birds singing in the treetops and the hedges.

Galloway twisted to study his companion. 'Just how big is Bennison?' he asked, and watched closely as Minden's expression changed subtly.

'A lot bigger than you give him credit for being,' said Minden. 'A lot bigger than almost anyone gives him credit for being. And I'll tell you frankly that I'd just as soon be shot right here as try entering that house of his with you, under the circumstances you have just outlined. Neither of us would ever make it back out again.'

12

One Riddle Resolved

Galloway did not question the veracity of Minden's generalizations, but being a practical man neither was he willing to be discouraged by them. As they sat at the kerbing he demanded specific facts.

'Okay, the house is a fortress. Does that mean the doors are steel and electronically operated, or does it mean that Bennison has guards inside?'

Minden squirmed. 'I told you that I've been in there, but I can't exactly pinpoint his protective devices. I didn't look for them, and Mister Bennison was with me all the while. I *do* know one thing — he had electric beams at every door and window. He told me that. He also has a floor-safe that is wired to electrocute anyone who tampers with it and does not know the combination.'

Galloway lit a cigarette, looked around

at the empty sidewalk and street, and looked back at Minden. 'How about guards?'

'Well; there was a butler. He brought drinks the evening I transacted business with Mister Bennison a couple of weeks ago. But I don't know whether he's actually a guard.'

'Anyone else?'

Minden got a pained expression across his face. 'I can't say. There must be a maid, but I didn't see her. There may be others, I really don't know. But you can't go in there even if there's only the butler, or whatever he is. Bennison didn't show me any more than I've told you, but the way he talked and acted I know for a fact there are other devices. Probably lethal ones.'

Galloway was not enthusiastic about going in there but as he blew smoke, he put it into the form of a question to Minden: 'Do you know of any other way to get those six paintings?'

Minden didn't. 'No. But they won't do you a bit of good if you're electrocuted, will they, and more to the point, if I'm electrocuted along with you.'

Galloway smiled. 'Then think of something.'

Minden was exasperated. 'Think of what? I've told you — there is no way to bring this off.'

Galloway put out his smoke in the dashboard ashtray and looked at his watch. The day was not quite half spent, but even so Galloway had already put in more than fifteen hours. Unless he wanted all that to go for nothing he had to think of something, and fairly soon because by now the police would be looking for the blue sport car.

'Bennison's the key,' he told Minden, 'drive until we find a public telephone then tell him you will meet him at his residence with some very important information about a fresh batch of valuable paintings from London.'

Minden looked pained. 'He is going to be very wary. Even if there were such a series of paintings, with the Mitreman thing still in the wind, I don't see anyone as shrewd as Mister Bennison wanting to get involved in anything like this.'

It was probably a good point. Galloway said, 'Make it tempting, Minden, and make it believable. I'll be at your side. These paintings can be bought at a ridiculously low price, and they are genuine Flemish masters worth a fortune.' Galloway pointed. 'Start the car and let's get about our little game.'

Minden started the car but he still looked pained. 'Why do I have to go in with you?' When Minden asked that he probably did not expect an answer, because when he did not get one he drove away without acting very surprised.

As for Galloway, he did not like the situation at all. If the police did not get him Bennison very likely would. Of the two, it was beginning to appear that the police would be preferable.

On the other hand, the situation had been progressing towards this moment ever since Galloway had listened to Inspector Merritt make that plea 'One last time.' Perhaps Galloway should have felt some grim elation. At least he knew who had the Bedford Gallery paintings, and he knew where they were. Actually, there only remained two moves to be made: Get the paintings, and leave the country. Everything else had been done.

As Minden pointed out a kerbside telephone kiosk, Galloway had a thought: There were *three* moves to be made, not two: Get the paintings, *stay alive*, and get the paintings out of the country.

Minden pulled to the kerbing and looked quizzically at his silent companion. Galloway jerked his head in the direction of the kiosk. They went over to it and Minden stepped inside. He knew the telephone number without looking it up, and to his credit he made the call and handled the conversation very creditably. Bennison did not agree to an immediate meeting, though. He said he was interested in what Minden had to tell him, but that he would be busy most of the afternoon and could not possibly meet Minden before five o'clock. He also wanted to know if he couldn't come by the North Camden Drive gallery and see the new art work. Minden hastily reported that the art work was not at his salon. He then said he'd meet Bennison at his residence after five and give him the particulars. Bennison seemed to hesitate briefly before agreeing, and after Minden put down the telephone Galloway had a hunch. As he motioned for Minden to return to the car, he looked around. If anyone had paid any attention to a pair of men using a public telephone they must have been watching from private, because no one on the street even faced that direction.

Galloway slid into the car and said, 'We're in trouble.'

Minden punched the starter and drove away. He said nothing until Galloway spoke again.

'I don't know whether it's because he knows you haven't been in your gallery, or whether he's got a pipeline into police headquarters and knows you are with me, but Mister Bennison was playing for time, and he was doing it like a man who detects an unpleasant odour.'

Minden drove slowly, heading back into the quiet residential area. 'He knows something is happening, I told you, Bennison is smart. If he called my office earlier they'd have told him I left with a stranger.'

There was nothing very incriminating in that, unless, as Galloway suspected, Bennison knew someone at police headquarters, and by now, the police knew exactly who it was that John Minden was with. They could have passed that along to Bennison, who in turn could have smelled the trap when Minden called him. Galloway should have anticipated this sticky situation; if he had, he could have seen to it that Minden mentioned him, the other Englishman, and made it seem that he, like Mitreman, had stolen paintings for sale. It might have sounded creditable.

Minden's anxiety drove him to make Galloway a proposition. 'Look; you're dragging me down with you. I know how this is going to end. Bennison is going to meet you after five o'clock this evening, three or four hours from now, and when you walk up, Bennison is going to have Tony Martinelli waiting for you. I'll make a trade with you: I have six paintings at my gallery that are just as valuable as the ones you are after. Take me back and I'll give them to you, then I'll go my way and you can go your way.'

Galloway smiled. 'Two flaws in that, Mister Minden. The most obvious one is that the moment either of us shows up at your gallery, the police will nab us. The other flaw is that I didn't come all that distance for substitute paintings.'

Minden groaned. 'You're going to get us both killed.'

Galloway did not refute that, he just did not dwell upon it at the moment, because something else Minden had said gave him a vague ray of hope. Bennison would meet them . . . *three or four hours from now.* That fit in fairly well with something else that had been in Galloway's thoughts. He said, 'Drive over close to Bennison's residence. Let's see if we can't find a decent place to hide this car.'

Minden obeyed but he protested. 'We're going to be on foot. Sitting ducks.'

Galloway, having already conceded that to himself, nodded pleasantly, and Minden, seeing his abductor's serene expression swore aloud.

'You're crazy. You're doing this all wrong, and you're setting us up like clay pigeons.'

'You are the noisiest clay pigeon I've ever seen,' asserted Galloway, and pointed as they came around the corner northward of Bennison's fenced-in estate. 'Nip into that alleyway.'

Minden obeyed, and the alleyway turned out to be one of those places where the garbage and refuse trucks called once a week to haul away trash. It was a fairly good place to leave the car, and better yet, Minden pulled into a vacant parking site just off the alleyway behind a high brick fence. There were already two cars parked there. The blue sport car made three and looked perfectly natural. As its passengers alighted, Minden loosened his tie and collar, came over beside Galloway and struck an adamant posture.

Before he could speak Galloway reached and gave him a light shove up the alleyway towards the northward tree-shaded quiet street. 'Just go along,' he told Minden. 'I know how you feel. I've been listening to you for a couple of hours and there's nothing more you can gripe about. Incidentally, if it'll make you feel any better, I'm not entirely enthusiastic about this mess either.'

Minden, moving ahead, said, 'Then forget it, because you're going to get yourself killed.'

Galloway did not argue, but when they reached the street he directed Minden right on past the access route towards the Bennison place, to the alleyway that was half a square beyond, and when Minden screwed up his face, Galloway tapped him lightly and shook his head.

'No more complaining, Mister Minden. I told you, I've heard all I want to hear. Just walk down the alleyway as though you had every right to do so.'

Bennison's house was not visible from the back alley. Like all the other exclusive residences in this area, there was a tall rear fence of either brick or fieldstone closing off visibility from the alleyway. But there was also a gate giving access to the Bennison grounds, and it was at this gate that Galloway halted, drawing Minden in with him as far as was necessary to look through.

The grounds between the rear wall and the back of the rambling, low house, were handsomely landscaped to give an impression of space confined by vigorous growth. There were several large trees and a number of flourishing hedges, set beyond a broad expanse of grass that looked as though it had very recently been clipped.

The house drowsed in tree-shade, its entire rear wall, windows and doorways, kept cool by long shadows. Minden said, 'Don't be fooled, it only *looks* easy.'

Galloway had no illusions. He looked at his wristwatch, looked at the electrical pole at his back in the alleyway, and turned to consider the open garage across the way, which formed a part of someone else's rear wall. 'Come along,' he said, and moved across towards that open garage.

Minden obeyed because by now he was more or less accustomed to it, but he looked blank as Galloway entered the opened garage and pointed to the lower end of a long ladder that was hanging on the wall there. Minden took that end,

Galloway took the narrow, upper end, and they carried the ladder back across the alleyway. As Galloway motioned for Minden to put the bottom of the ladder against the base of the rear wall at the Bennison property, Minden said, 'What in the hell is this all about? You can walk through that back gate, you don't have to climb the wall.'

Galloway did not answer. He went back, heaved the ladder upright, balanced it carefully and finally let it drop over against the power pole. Minden, understanding that at least the idea was not to climb the ladder to get atop the wall, still looked slightly baffled.

Galloway tested the ladder, then turned and pointed. 'Go stand across the way, over in front of that open garage. Don't try to come over here and dump the ladder, and don't do anything as stupid as trying to run down the alleyway. From up there I can pot-shot you like a grouse. Go over there!'

Minden obeyed, and he watched with frank interest while Galloway ran up the rungs. Dealers in art rarely knew much about electricity, and it was plain that John Minden was equally as baffled by *why*, as well as *what*, Galloway was up to.

At the top of the power pole, or at least close to its top, was the round, battleship-grey transformer. To one side of the transformer were three round, long, red-coloured high-power fuses. Each one operated on an overload-ejector; if a surge of power hit the fuses they would automatically break away to prevent the expensive transformer from burning out. When they broke away, the supply of power was stopped from reaching the transformer.

Those fuses were also easy to grasp and pull loose, and that was what Galloway did. One at a time, he disengaged each fuse, put it atop the transformer, then came back down to the ground, told Minden to lend a hand lowering the ladder, and the other thought that had occurred to Galloway had been implemented.

Every protective device Minden had told Galloway about since early morning had been electrically-operated. Now, there was no electricity reaching the Bennison residence at all. Not even enough to operate a doorbell.

And Galloway still had three or four hours!

13

A Matter of Paintings

Minden had some idea of what Galloway had done. At least the fact that by disengaging those fuses Galloway had stopped electricity from entering the transformer, which fed the lines going to the Bennison residence, was rather apparent. As Minden helped lower the ladder he said, 'The servants will telephone Mister Bennison or the electricity people.'

Galloway nodded and walked over to the side of Bennison's garage where a round aluminium cylinder at head-height, fed two ingoing wires and two outgoing ones. He twisted the cylinder until the sheathing loosened, then tore loose two wires. 'No telephone,' he said.

Minden looked puzzled. He did not speak but obviously he was impressed. When he turned to crane around towards the house, Galloway said, 'My army speciality was communications.' He gestured for Minden to walk through into the rear garden of the Bennison residence. At the same time Galloway loosened his jacket with an unmistakable meaning, and Minden turned to obey.

It was an unrealistic situation; there were birds in the treetops, a bright sun burning through grey smog, daylight heat except in the shady places they passed, and the house looked as friendly and inviting as any house had ever looked, and yet there was probably about an even chance that neither Galloway nor John Minden were going to live to leave that house. At least that had been Minden's paean ever since breakfast time. Now, though, he walked ahead and said nothing.

On the other hand, Galloway had an idea that he had cut the odds by eliminating the electricity. There was one thing worrying him, over and above getting out of this alive: That floor-safe Minden had mentioned. If Bennison had those six paintings stored in that thing, even though Galloway had eliminated the danger of electrocution, how could the safe be opened? It was very unlikely that Howard Bennison entrusted the combination to a butler or a maid, and Galloway was helpless when it came to opening safes. He had his capabilities, but safe-breaking was definitely not one of them.

By the time he and Minden reached the back of the house Galloway had his mind made up. If the paintings were in that blasted safe he was simply going to have to sit in there and wait until Bennison arrived — probably with his hired killer, Tony Martinelli.

Minden looked over his shoulder with a hand raised to punch the door bell. Galloway shook his head. 'Walk right in.' Minden obeyed. They were in a rather large service porch. Beyond was a gleaming kitchen. No one was in sight as Minden led the way on through and halted at the archway leading into a butler's pantry. Beyond this there was a swinging door that obviously led into the dining-room. Galloway delayed Minden until he had his ugly-barrelled handgun in his fist, then nodded. Minden, without looking at all pleased, pushed past the swinging door, and two people whirled. One was a burly man dressed in a houseboy's white coat, and the other was a middle-aged, vinegary-faced woman who was wiping her hands on a small towel. She kept right on doing this even when she sprang her eyes wide open in astonishment when she saw Galloway and the gun.

The burly man gazed from Minden to Galloway, and back. 'Mister Minden,' he said, in a dry, somewhat harsh tone of voice. He looked at the gun. 'I hope you know what you are doing, Mister Minden.'

To Galloway, the burly man sent a cold, calculating look and pursed his lips in dogged silence. If he was simply a houseboy or butler as Minden had implied, he was certainly built more like a wrestler, and right at this moment, looked more like a strongarm man. Galloway told the man to shed his white jacket. There was no hesitation at all, even though the shoulder-holster and its dark-butted contents were exposed. The house-boy seemed to expect nothing less than to be disarmed. Galloway obliged him, had Minden take the gun and pass it back — butt first — then Galloway told Minden to lead the procession and take them all to the floor safe.

No one spoke. The maid had stopped drying her bone-dry hands but she clung to the towel like a child would cling to a blanket.

The safe was beneath a large rug in the stone floor of the elegant study, about where Galloway would have guessed it might be. One long look and Galloway knew he was definitely in trouble. Assuming the paintings were down inside that mass of stone, cement, and rein-forced steel, Galloway's only option was to wait until Bennison arrived, and hope for the best, although obviously Bennison would not arrived unprepared.

He could feel the chill closing in around his heart. The odds were stacking up again. He asked the burly butler when was the last time anyone had opened that safe, and got a mean smile and a stalwart head-shake. 'I don't know. That's out of bounds for everyone but the boss. I never even seen inside the thing.' The man's small, malevolent eyes brightened. 'That's it,' he suddenly exclaimed. 'That's why there's no electricity. You guys cut it off to get a crack at the safe.' The burly man swung his head towards John Minden, his malevolence more noticeable than ever. 'Mister Minden, you sure played hell this time. He'll fix your little red wagon sure as hell — but *good* — for this.'

Minden started to protest, but Galloway cut across the sound with a question to the burly man. 'Is this the only safe?'

The burly man's narrowed eyes lingered speculatively on Galloway, and dropped once to the unwavering gun before the malevolent smile broadened. 'You go right ahead and guess, mister. I'm not going to tell you anything.'

Galloway met the mean smile with a colder one, and cocked the gun. John Minden and the frightened maid stiffened. It may have been that, or it may have been the cold smile, but the burly man relented.

'There's another one in the master bedroom.'

Galloway gestured with the gun. 'Lead the way. Act heroic and maybe they'll inscribe that on your tombstone.'

The master bedroom, as it turned out, adjoined the study, and although there had been some rather good paintings in the study, because its panelled walls were mostly covered with bookshelves, the art work did not predominate, but the master bedroom which was quite commodious even by Brentwood standards, being, Galloway estimated about twenty feet square, had what were probably Bennison's best paintings on all four walls, and when Minden faltered as he entered the room, looking over above the great mahogany bedstead, Galloway's gaze quickened. But those three paintings over there hanging side by side did not impress Galloway, although he was willing to concede that no one would ever seek his services as an art critic.

He had spent the entire previous night surrounded by masterful, and soulful, art, and had only liked two rather mundane paintings.

The burly butler opened a clothes-closet door, moved aside some suits hanging from the rack and disclosed a circular wall-safe. He waited for some comment from Galloway, and got none as Galloway leaned on the wall beside the door leading into the bedroom from the study.

That second safe meant no more than the larger one in the stone floor meant, unless Minden, the maid, or the burly butler, knew how to open it. None of them did, because Galloway asked, and got three vehement headshakes that were very convincing.

'Aside from safes,' said Galloway to the burly man, 'where does Mister Bennison keep valuables?'

The butler gestured with both arms. 'The whole house is full of 'em. Every painting is valuable. Ask Minden there, he sold most of them to Mister Bennison.'

Minden winced, then avoided Galloway's look.

'Even the furniture is very old and very valuable stuff. Mister Bennison only buys valuable things. If you got an eye for that kind of stuff look around you. That bedstead, for instance, cost more'n I make in two years. It come from Monticello, Thomas Jefferson's home.' The burly man went on giving a running inventory of valuables and it dawned on Galloway why he was doing this: To stall, to delay Galloway until someone arrived. He may have had certain knowledge that someone was due to arrive, or he may only have been stalling to gain time in the hope that someone *might* arrive, but in either case Galloway had no intention of being kept there any longer than was absolutely necesary.

He told the butler to shut up, then turned on John Minden. 'Where are the other three paintings?'

Minden blinked. 'Other *three*? I thought you wanted all six.'

Galloway gestured towards the far wall with his revolver. 'Those are three of them, Minden. Care to deny it?'

Minden turned with noticeable reluctance and looked again at the paintings he had first seen when he'd entered the room, and had faltered about. 'I have no idea where the other three are,' he said sulkily, and Galloway moved away from the door towards him.

He gestured with the gun. 'Take those three off the wall and carry them along. Butler; take us on a tour until we find the other three.'

For the first time the maid opened her mouth. She was an ugly, horse-faced, angular woman, flat and sinewy and probably very efficient because there couldn't be any other reason why an employer, especially a bachelor employer, would have kept her.

'The day Mister Bennison hung those three paintings he hung another three out in the solarium.' She turned fully to face Galloway. 'Mister, if those are the pictures you want, will you take them and go right away?'

Galloway felt like smiling. 'If the other three are the ones I'm after, madam, I'll be delighted to take them and go.' He

167

motioned for the burly man to lead out. 'To the solarium, and you had better hope we have three winners out there.' As the maid and butler moved, Galloway laid a restraining hand on John Minden's arm and raised his eyebrows. 'Are you certain these three are the ones we're after?'

Minden scowled and nodded. 'I sold them to him, didn't I? I'm very certain.'

Minden followed the other two out of the room and Galloway brought up the rear as they crossed a sunken, very elaborate sitting-room and stepped up one step to emerge into a place that was almost like a greenhouse in that it had indoors shrubbery along three walls, and glass windows full length, and even part way up the roofline. Three walls were arranged to allow late-day afternoon sunshine in. The fourth wall, which was a rear segment of the house-proper, rose to a high ceiling. On this wall Galloway, who was watching Minden closely, saw the other three paintings. Appropriately enough they were of landscapes. Galloway liked them for that reason. Otherwise they did not look especially outstanding. The fact that they were the only paintings out there, on the solarium wall, and had very clearly been hung out there only very recently, left the question of their significance answered, without Minden's verification. Galloway watched the art-dealer put the three paintings he had brought from the master bedroom aside, gently, and motion for the butler to lend a hand at removing the three framed works of art on the stone wall. The burly man did not make any of his bleak threats, for a change, as he helped Minden get the paintings down, but afterwards, when Galloway was considering the six large frames, the burly man stole a sneaky look at his wristwatch.

Galloway saw that. He also knew that so far he had only used up an hour and a half of the three or four hours, so he was not too upset, although there of course was a possibility that Bennison, or some-one he might send along like Tony Martinelli, might be arriving any moment, but Gallo-way had always more or less lived with uncertainty. He accepted it now as he gave John Minden an order.

'Break those frames and take the canvases out.'

Minden recoiled. 'I have no tools.'

Galloway was unsmiling as he said, 'Do it, or I'll split your skull, and do it damned fast.'

Minden broke into a noticeable sweat as he turned on the first painting. He looked helplessly at the burly man and the maid, but they did not seem the least bit concerned about the welfare of the art. Their predominant interest was in Galloway's ugly-snouted revolver.

Minden proved that his protest had not been valid by working loose a jointed, glued corner of the first frame without much actual effort, and afterwards stripping away the backing and the wood without any risk to the painting. He worked surely and rapidly; obviously, this close to the conclusion of what he had been forced to come here and help accomplish, Minden wanted to get it over with. He probably realized that there was actually a fair chance of his coming out of this alive after all.

14

The Next Step

The burly man, watching Minden's swift progress, said, 'You guys won't get away with this. Not a chance in the world of it.'

Galloway was unimpressed by the threat but his unwilling cohort, working swiftly and a little shakily, seemed impressed. He dropped two paintings and cursed as he had to bend and retrieve them. The maid was still clinging to her small towel, and although no one paid any attention to her, she appeared to believe she was in some kind of imminent peril. As Minden finished removing the fourth painting from its frame she said, 'I'm going to quit. I knew better than to ever go to work for Mister Bennison anyway.'

The butler growled at her. 'Shut up, Aimee.'

It might have worked another time, but

not now. The maid glowered and said, 'Who are you to tell me to shut up; what do you ever do around here, anyway, except scowl at people and act like a butler in a blundering way?'

The burly man coloured and turned mean. 'I said shut up. That's what I meant.'

Galloway waved the gun at the burly man. 'Let her have her say.'

But the maid subsided. She looked as though she could have gone on speaking for another ten minutes, but she seemed to realize that, short of getting it off her very flat chest, whatever she said was not going to help her in any way. She went to a chair and sat down, still clutching the small towel. She only made one other comment, and that was after Minden was rolling the six paintings carefully into a cylindrical shape.

Pointing to the broken, scattered frames she said, 'Just look at that mess!'

Galloway looked. So did everyone else, when she said that, because her tone had been impelling. Minden had ruined six rather ornate and probably rather expensive picture frames. He had ruined them in such a way that wood and splinters, canvas backing and shreds of it, were scattered over a sofa, a chair, and the flagstone, highly-polished solarium floor.

Galloway herded them all back to the kitchen, and here, for the first time, the burly man looked tense and anxious. He had good reason; the robbery had been successfully completed, the maid and the burly man were the only witnesses, the only ones who could raise an alarm.

Galloway rummaged a dozen kitchen drawers before finding what he sought, a roll of freeze-proof gummed paper, the kind used by householders when they wrapped meat for the deep-freeze. He tossed it to Minden and motioned towards the burly man. 'And don't forget his mouth,' said Galloway, mirthlessly smiling.

The burly man recoiled when Minden approached him. He balled up a fist and kept it hanging out of sight. Galloway waited until Minden was within a foot of the burly man, then tilted the gunbarrel as he said, 'You so much as open your mouth, and you'll never be that lucky again.'

Minden and the burly man exchanged a look, then Minden turned the man with one hand, and taped his wrists together behind his back. After that, he did the same with the burly man's ankles, and finally, he taped his mouth closed, going completely around the head half a dozen times. It was actually a far better job than Galloway had expected. Ever since they had left the car and had entered the Bennison grounds, Minden's dependence upon Galloway had seemed to be strengthening.

The maid submitted with the expression of Joan of Arc going to the stake and Minden finished with her in half the time. There was no need for either the maid or the butler being made unnecessarily uncomfortable. Even if they worked free of the tape, the telephone was still out of order.

Galloway told Minden to move out ahead of him with the rolled-up paintings, then he stood in the doorway watching. Minden did not like that. When Galloway caught up half-way across the rear garden Minden glared at him.

'And suppose someone like Martinelli had been out here?'

Galloway smiled. 'You'd probably be dead.'

In the alleyway again, Galloway took a southerly course. He had no intention of going back where they had left the blue car. Minden was worrying again about being on foot. He was one of those people to whom any kind of escape involved wheels. He did not like being the one to carry the rolled-up paintings, either, although his complaint was neither very forceful nor very convincing.

The streets were quiet, there was scarcely any traffic, even a brown delivery van going by caught and held the attention of the two men walking out of the alleyway. The van slewed to the kerbing, a brown-uniformed driver sprang out and went hurrying towards a distant house carrying a package. Galloway sighed, nudged Minden, and they went up on the blind side of the van, got in, and Minden handed over the paintings as he engaged gears and drove off.

'If I don't get five-to-ten for grand theft

auto it will be a miracle,' he said, over the noisy sounds of the delivery van. 'Where are we going now?'

Galloway settled comfortably upon a small jump-seat holding the rolled-up paintings, and said, 'That's entirely up to you.'

Minden missed the implication, and quite understandably since he had no idea how Galloway's mind was working. 'In that case I'd like nothing better than to separate from you.'

Galloway said nothing until they had crossed a fairly busy intersection and although he looked closely, he saw no police cruisers. So far so good. He looked in the back of the van, found plenty of wrapping paper, and went back there to make a solid bundle of the six paintings. He even found a heavy cardboard cylinder. It had someone else's goods in it but it only took a moment to put them aside. There was plenty of tape and cord. When he had finished wrapping the bundle he stepped back up front, rummaged a jockey-box for a pen, addressed the package and, with Minden craning to try and see to whom the package had been addressed, Galloway turned it face down on his lap and ordered Minden to find a post-office.

He also took Minden in with him when he posted the package, and Minden never did get to see the address. But it cost a sizeable sum to pay the postage, so Minden could hardly have avoided an inkling that the paintings were being posted out of the country. He probably would have been astonished if he'd discovered they were being mailed to a London police inspector.

When they were back in the van Minden froze when a black-and-white police car cruised past. Afterwards, he let his breath out in a hiss, and told Galloway they were going to have to get rid of the van.

Galloway was willing. He said, 'Any ideas where we'll find a successor?'

Minden lit a cigarette, rolled up his eyes, and shook his head. 'No. And I've done everything I could, or should, have done for you. We're going to have to split up now.'

Galloway smiled. 'What! And only because I got the bloody pictures back.'

Minden looked surprised. 'What else?'

'The money,' said Galloway, and Minden stared as though he hadn't believed his ears. 'The money Bennison paid you for them, Mister Minden, and which you did not deposit. On the assumption that it's at your house, suppose we drive over there.'

Minden started the van, then looked up quickly. 'They'll have it under surveillance.'

'How about the gallery then.'

Minden screwed up his face. 'You know perfectly well both places are hot for either of us.'

'Then let's go wherever you've put the money.'

Minden swung the van around a blind corner, nearly hit a pedestrian, and ignored the string of obscenities to say, 'I'll take you to the airport, and swear to say nothing. You can shoot me if you like, but you're not going to get a cent of that money!'

Galloway did not press the issue. He

told Minden to drive the van down close to the Beverly Hilton Hotel, where they would abandon it. Galloway's thinking was that while the police would realize the hotel was not excessively far from Minden's gallery, they might also be interested in the van being found where Mitreman's corpse had also been found. It wasn't much, really, in the way of a diversion, but Galloway was satisfied with it. From now on his strategy had to encompass constant movement and avoidance of crossing his own tracks. As long as the police were *chasing*, were only two or three steps behind on a hot trail, they would probably not try *anticipating*.

Minden chose to halt the van in a press of other parked vehicles behind the hotel and not far from the service entrance. He and Galloway walked away from it as though they had every right in the world to be casual, but their conversation was anything but casual.

Galloway said they would wait until evening then enter the gallery the same way he had entered it the previous night, and Minden had two objections. One, was based on the grounds that there would be no way to approach his building, now, and not be seen by police surveillance teams. The other objection was that it was pointless to return to his gallery.

Galloway was sympathetic but adamant. 'I've really done what I came here to accomplish. The paintings will be out of the country by midnight. If the police nail me now I can become reconciled to the delay, because actually they don't have too much on me. Not like they have on you.'

Minden did not argue about this. 'Why do you think I'd rather not go back to the salon?'

Galloway smiled as they strode through the hot afternoon. 'Probably to avoid being apprehended,' he said, 'and also to avoid taking me where the money is hidden.'

Minden faltered in his stride. 'At my gallery? Do I look that simple-minded?'

'You look that shrewd,' stated Galloway. 'The gallery would be better than your house. After all, Martinelli may like music, but you'd have a hell of a time convincing me that was why he was in your house — to listen to the stereo. Martinelli must be a capable double-crosser himself. If he took Mitreman out for you, then he knows *why* it had to be done, and that means he also knows you have the money.'

Minden shoved fisted hands into trouser pockets and trudged along scowling. Whatever was troubling him had evidently been in his mind for some time. After a moment of hard thought, he said, 'Martinelli wasn't in my house with permission, but I've already told you that, haven't I?'

Galloway nodded.

'Well; when you told me he was there, the picture began to emerge, and Martinelli is only a small part of it. It's Bennison: He also knows how much money I got because he paid it to me. Somehow, probably through the bank's officers, he must have learned, as you also did, that I didn't deposit that money. Now do you understand why Martinelli was waiting in my house without my knowledge?'

Galloway looked at Minden. This was something he had not considered. 'To get the money back,' he said, 'and kill you.'

Minden shrugged. 'To get the money, I'm positive. About the rest — I don't know.'

Galloway said, 'I know. Martinelli told Bennison that you were the one who turned him in to the police. He was pretty upset about that; wanted revenge against you. Bennison told him to come see him at his office and not to do anything until he'd seen him.'

Minden raised sceptical eyes. 'How do you know all this?'

'Off a taped telephone conversation between them I found in Bennison's office.' Galloway slowed as they came to North Camden Drive. 'Suppose the police aren't the only ones watching the gallery.' He changed course and turned Minden around with him. 'I know where there's a quiet old rooming-house. We'd better go wait for darkness over there. The idea of Bennison's client, Mister Martinelli, waiting at your desk in the gallery, or perhaps in some shop across the street, with his silenced gun, takes a lot of the fun out of all this for me.'

Minden did not argue when they walked off in a different direction through the heavy pedestrian traffic, but he looked a good bit more worn and weary than he had looked earlier in the day. No doubt about it, John Minden had just spent one of the most adventuresome and hectic days of his lifetime. But he was still free, and most important of all, he was still alive.

Galloway was none too certain how much longer he would be able to maintain this *status quo*, but he had a very strong incentive to do it; he only lacked one thing, then he could try and devise some way of flying home although undoubtedly every airport would by now also be under surveillance for the second Englishman. He only lacked the money.

15

A Matter of Money

Minden had evidently accepted his subordinate position with Galloway without reservations. At least he was acting that way when the pair of them entered the rooming-house, although there was one point he did not seem willing to even discuss, let alone consider a compromise over: The money.

When Galloway offered him a smoke, then lit up for them both as he said, 'Make your mind up to it, I'm not leaving without the money any more than I'd have left without the paintings,' Minden inhaled, exhaled, went to a chair and planted himself over there with a look of iron-like unrelenting stubbornness.

'Then you'd better take out citizenship papers, Limey, because there's not a prayer of you getting a cent of it.'

Galloway did not wave the weapon. He

was not only averse to bluffing, just on general principles, he was also convinced from having spent the day with John Minden and having learned something about the man, that threats were not going to make it with him.

He smiled, went to stand by a dingy window looking down at the tree-shaded quiet back-street, and said, 'I think you left it at the bank.'

'Guess all you want,' exclaimed Minden. 'You also thought it was at my residence.'

Galloway turned, shaking his head. 'Not on second thought. You weren't upset enough when you learned Martinelli had been inside the house, probably ransacking it.'

Minden smiled. 'Very good. Now deduce a reason for it not being in the gallery.'

Galloway laughed and said, 'I'm not so sure it isn't there. I've got an idea how to prove it, one way or the other.'

Galloway's humour was lost on Minden, who smoked, watched his companion through narrowed, respecting eyes, and said nothing although he was obviously far from being speechless.

'Tonight,' said Galloway, 'I'm going to burn the place.'

Minden started to his feet. 'The gallery? What the hell kind of gawd-damned stupidity is that?'

'Vindictiveness,' said Galloway, candidly. 'If I don't get the money, then neither do you.'

'Money my neck,' snapped Minden. 'The damned money is not at my gallery — but you'll destroy three-quarters of a million dollars worth of valuable art if you burn the salon.'

Galloway's humour lingered. 'Terrible decision to have to make, what? Look, Mister Minden, I'll prove that I'm a reasonable man. I won't take the entire two hundred and twenty-five thousand. You'll need money to get away, and a little to get re-established wherever you land. Keep fifty thousand and give me the rest. One hundred and seventy-five thousand dollars will enable me to — '

'You're crazy!' exclaimed Minden.

Galloway paused, considered his associate, and slowly wagged his head. 'You're

186

not being at all practical, are you? Isn't it better to escape with fifty thousand dollars than not to escape at all?' Galloway pointed to the wall-telephone. 'For five cents I can fix it so that you won't even get to spend the fifty thousand. Bennison ought to be very interested in your whereabouts, by now. It's well past five o'clock. He's seen that wreckage you left in the solarium where you removed the frames. I judge Mister Bennison to be a very irascible individual, Mister Minden. Now, he is not only out the two hundred and twenty-five thousand dollars, but he is also out the six paintings. His kind of a man can't possibly rest when he's been used that badly. He probably wouldn't even wait for Martinelli to hit you, because Martinelli is still under police surveillance. That means, Mister Minden, that you wouldn't recognize the killer, would you?'

Minden's stubbornness lingered. 'Nor would you. After all, we're in this together. It was you who master-minded that burglary.'

'But Bennison doesn't know me by

sight, Mister Minden, and even if he did, my intention is to be very certain he doesn't find me. You — I can leave you right here in this room, unconscious, make the telephone call, and be long gone by the time his killer comes up the stairs and walks in on you.'

Minden took a final inhalation of his cigarette, stubbed it out in a metal ashtray near at hand, blew smoke and stalked over to the front window to look out. 'You are just talking,' he growled, without turning to look at Galloway. He did not sound convinced, nor, actually, did he have much cause to feel that way. Any way he thought about it, this was Morton Galloway's ball game. Galloway had engineered it this way, and, like it or not, Minden had to see the facts as they were: He was trapped. Not only between Bennison, who would by now be in a frothing fury, and Martinelli, who would want Minden alive just long enough to squeeze out of him where the money was cached, but also between the various police agencies who wanted Minden very badly, by now, in relation to a murder over at the Beverly-Hilton hotel.

Finally, there was the Englishman.

Minden did not even know Galloway's name, which wasn't any enormity, but it signified to him that whoever Galloway was, he was certainly no novice, and if this was no consolation, there was one very faint glimmer for Minden: Galloway was his only hope. He was not experienced enough, by himself, to break free from the tightening enclosure.

'Fifty thousand dollars,' he told Galloway. 'In exchange for that you have to guarantee to get me out of the country.'

Galloway stood gazing at his companion in quiet thought. Then he shook his head. 'I wouldn't even guarantee to get you out of Los Angeles for fifty thousand dollars.'

'You have a high opinion of yourself,' growled Minden.

Galloway did not deny this. 'If you want to try it the inexpensive way, call a taxi. The minute you do that, I'll call Bennison. You'll have a sporting chance. If Bennison doesn't get you perhaps the police will, or perhaps Martinelli. Not such terribly good odds at that, are they: Three to one.'

'Fifty thousand dollars is exceptional pay for all you've done to earn it here in the States. And then there are the paintings, which you have no doubt posted to your collaborator in Europe. You'll get a quarter of a million over there, I'm sure, or its equivalent.'

Galloway glanced at his wristwatch, glanced out of a window where the shadows were lengthening, and said no more for as long as it took him to go through the routine of ascertaining how much time he had, before nightfall would enable him to leave the protection of the rooming-house. That seemed to trouble Minden because he fidgetted, moving from the window to the door, then over where the telephone hung on the wall, and finally back to the chair he'd used earlier. He also lit another cigarette and snapped the match before dropping it in the metal ashtray.

'What in the hell do I get out of this,' he demanded of Galloway, 'if I hand over more than fifty thousand dollars to you?'

Galloway shrugged, looking uncon-cerned. 'I've already explained that to you, Mister Minden: You probably get to stay alive.'

'I'll stay alive anyway,' muttered Minden, blowing more smoke and looking slightly more desperate. 'Why can't you be satis-fied with the paintings and fifty thousand dollars?'

'I'm greedy,' confessed Galloway, mildly.

'Seventy-five thousand, Limey, and by gawd not one cent more!'

Galloway looked out at the descending dusk again and ignored his companion as he turned and strolled over to lean upon the wall beside the telephone, staring at Minden without making a sound.

The silence between them drew out taut. Minden fished through his pockets for another smoke and came up with only a crumpled empty packet which he hurled in the direction of a cheap, dark wooden dresser.

Galloway drew out his own packet and tossed it over. As Minden caught it Galloway said, 'When the daylight ends out there, Mister Minden, we are both going out of here. You wanted to separate, well, that's what we're going to do. And each one of us will have about ten hours of nice darkness to try and get clear — except that you are going to have a handicap: I've decided to call not only Bennison, but also the police, and tell them where you were — in this room — and that you are trying to get out of the city. You'll have ten hours of darkness to escape them, and they'll have the same ten hours to find you.' Galloway waited until Minden had the cigarette lighted before concluding what he had to say. 'I think I'll bet on the police beating Bennison and his killers to you.'

'Martinelli and Bennison are penny-ante double-crossers compared to you,' snarled Minden.

Galloway defended himself. 'I'm not double-crossing you because I've never been on your side. To me, Mister Minden, you've never been anything but the key to a riddle — where the paintings were. As far as I'm concerned, you're no better than the man you hired to kill Mitreman. Double-cross you?' Galloway gave a hard little short laugh. 'I'm simply offering you some alternatives, just like any businessman would do, except that I'm offering you your life in exchange for some money you're not going to live to spend otherwise.'

'There's no way you can guarantee I'll be safe,' growled Minden.

Galloway conceded that. 'Probably not. But I'll guarantee you one thing, Mister Minden: If I *don't* get the money, you are dead.' Galloway smiled. 'That is what I'll guarantee you.'

For John Minden defeat was a blind alley and he must have recognized it, but also, two hundred and twenty-five thousand dollars was enough, more than enough, if he could escape with it intact, to go somewhere a long way off and start over again. The choice was not at all easy. Galloway, standing against the wall eyeing Minden, conceded to himself in private that he wouldn't have found it easy to make the decision either.

But he didn't have to decide, and he wasn't bluffing. To Galloway, John Minden was nothing more and nothing less than a substitute for Mitreman, Galloway's mortal enemy whom Minden had hired killed. Galloway could very easily transfer his animus for one to the other, exactly as he could rationalize his having earned the two hundred and twenty-five thousand dollars by being imprisoned for two years as a result of Mitreman's scheming. Mitreman's American associate, John Minden, was the inheritor of Mitreman's legacy of dishonesty. To Galloway, this kind of rationalization was easy.

He stood slouched and easy, waiting with quiet patience for Minden to make the decision, and meanwhile, just beyond the windows, dusk was falling. Dusk was the hour-glass, when it blotted out the last daylight, Galloway had to move. He did not propose to stay in Beverly Hills, in California, in the States, one more moment than he had to, and that meant he expected to be airborne no later than the following morning.

Minden punched out his cigarette and stamped over to the window, looked down into the gloomy street with his hands pocketed, with his shoulders hunched, with an expression of pitch-black exasperation across his face, and Galloway thought that it was probably a very good thing that Minden was not carrying a revolver too; he was not, normally at least, the killing kind, but Minden was certainly in a position now where he would kill, if it was in him at all to do that.

He swung away from the window and glared. 'Half the money. Half of two hundred and twenty-five thousand, Limey. That's enough for you to live like a lord for one hell of a long while. If you refuse, I'm walking out of here right now, and you can call the cops and Howard Benni-son, and anyone else you care to. I'll tell you honestly that I'm losing a lot more; the minute I fly out of this country I've sacrificed my art gallery, all the years I've worked building up my reputation as a —'

'Save all that,' cut in Galloway, 'because you'll be back in business within a month or two somewhere else. You are a very adaptable person, Mister Minden, I'm familiar with your type. As for the offer . . . ' Galloway deliberately paused and let the silence run out long and thin before speaking again. 'You can keep seventy-five thousand. The rest you will hand to me.' He pointed to the untouched bed. 'Put it over there on the counterpane.' He smiled at Minden. 'I should have guessed sooner, shouldn't I have? A moment ago you said it wasn't at the bank, the house, the gallery. That rather well eliminated most of the places a careful man would trust that much money — except for perhaps wrapped round his own middle under his clothing.'

Minden made no denial, but he said, 'Your word you will take only what you're entitled to?'

Galloway sighed in exaggerated resignation. 'One hundred and fifty thousand dollars, Mister Minden, and I don't mind telling you that I'm being very badly paid for risking my life. All right, count it out over there on the bed. Then we'd better give some thought to getting out of the country.'

16

Minden's Options

Galloway had got himself involved in something he never, under ordinary circumstances, would have touched with a ten-foot pole. Galloway had always been a loner. If he'd ever considered taking someone along when he was actively employed in his speciality, it most certainly would never have been when he was running-desperate.

But that was exactly what he had more or less consented to burden himself with now. He picked up the packet of smokes Minden had left on a table, lit one, watched the other man clawing inside his waistband, and went moodily over to look out the front window. Not only was Galloway giving away a great amount of money he did not actually have to give away, but he was saddling himself with a fugitive from justice who would be about as valuable and helpful on a run for life as a small child.

He thought of Inspector Merritt. *One last time*. He felt like swearing.

Minden called and pointed to the large notes lying atop the counterpane. 'A hundred and fifty thousand, Limey. That's the easiest money you ever made.'

Galloway strolled over, reached out pleasantly and stabbed Minden's chest with a bony finger. 'Call me Limey just one more time,' he said, smilingly affably, all but his eyes. 'And for your edification, Mister Minden, one hundred and fifty thousand dollars is peanuts.' He pushed Minden away, leaned and picked up some of the money to be counted. It took a little time, and outside the rooming-house night was falling. Minden went to the window and looked out, made certain, then went back over to the bed where Galloway was completing the counting. 'All there?' asked Minden, and Galloway nodded his head without answering while he stuffed a fortune into several pockets.

Minden seemed to recover rapidly from having to part with all that money. He went over to pocket the packet of smokes and stand by the door. 'All right, master-mind, let's see you conjure up a magic carpet and whisk us out of this mess.'

Galloway could smile because his clothing was nicely padded with green-backs. It did nothing for the hang of either jacket or trousers, but if a man had to look a bit baggy and shapeless, that was the ideal source for it.

Galloway went to the door, opened it, and as he led the way on out of the building he said, 'A taxi for starters, Mister Minden, and from this moment on, we're walking bulls-eyes again.'

When they reached the dark, warm night out front, Minden was interested in where they would go by taxi, and Galloway said truthfully that he was more concerned in keeping on the move than he was in a particular location, just yet. That seemed to sit well with Minden, but he did not look as though he understood it.

They did not find a cab until they had reached Wilshire Boulevard, and even then they had to walk all the way down to a hack-stand where cabbies idled away standby time in a small enclave reserved exclusively for them.

Minden acted the part of a mute. Even after they were both in a cab heading easterly towards Los Angeles from Beverly Hills, Minden sat in back beside Galloway, and said nothing. They had to stop once at a liquor store so Galloway could go inside and purchase several packets of cigarettes. Their driver was a young man, uninterested in his fares, who concentrated on the early-night traffic, which was moderately heavy for the middle of the week; nearer the end of each week there was more nightlife traffic heading towards the city's fleshpots from places like Beverly Hills, but for some reason this mid-week night was almost as busy.

John Minden made a comment about this, and Galloway listened politely and said nothing. He wasn't the least bit concerned.

So far, Galloway had been successful at walking the knife's edge. So far he had been able to stay ahead primarily because, until very recently, no one knew who he was. But that was obviously past now. He was just as much a hunted fugitive as was his companion. From here on — and Galloway was very aware of it — if he out-smarted the police and Howard Bennison, it would have to be without the advantage he'd had before.

He knew the main secret of remaining free. It was constant, and if possible unpredictable, movement. If he stopped again, between now and daylight, for as long as he had waited back there in that rooming-house for nightfall to descend, he would very probably be apprehended. When a man was being pursued the most fatal mistake he could make was to crouch down somewhere and hope the pursuit would rush on past.

There was just one thing left for Galloway to do, and indubitably it was going to prove the most difficult of everything he had accomplished up to now: Escape from the country.

For a while it might have been possible for Galloway to nonchalantly book a flight out of Los Angeles Municipal Airport by only using another name. Now, that was no longer possible. Even if he hadn't had John Minden with him, it wouldn't have been possible. By now the police had his description, and they didn't even have to go to London to get it. That car-rental would have it on record, and also by now, the police would have interviewed the landlord of the first place where Galloway had stayed after arriving in Beverly Hills.

The cab driver cut across Galloway's thoughts with a short question: 'Where to, mister, or do you boys just want to ride around?'

Minden turned mute again, gazing at Galloway. For the space of a hundred feet or so Galloway did not answer, then he leaned and asked if the driver knew where the Santa Susanna airport was, over in Simi Valley, the next farthest valley beyond Los Angeles after the San Fernando Valley. The driver knew, but he looked surprised. 'Mister, you know how much a drive over there in a cab will cost?'

Galloway smiled. 'No. Why don't you drive us out there, so we can find out?'

The driver looked at his two fares in the rearview mirror, evidently decided they were well-enough dressed to stand the tariff, and settled squarely behind his steering-wheel for the two-hour drive.

Minden leaned and said, 'You're not the stranger hereabouts I thought you were. Mind telling me why the Simi Valley airport?'

'I don't mind at all,' murmured Galloway. 'Can you give me one good reason why we wouldn't both be arrested the moment we walked into Burbank or L.A. International airports?'

Minden nodded. 'But why Simi Valley?'

Galloway curbed a short answer. 'Because we are not going to fly out of Los Angeles, and we are not going to fly *into* it, until we've gone somewhere else.'

Minden was interested. 'All right, but the best we can manage at Simi Airport is a small carrier, and usually they go north, not south.'

Galloway's patience was slipping. 'Relax, Mister Minden. When we get to Portland you'll have plenty to worry about.' Galloway nodded in the direction of their driver. He had kept his voice low, but it wasn't just that the driver might be able to say where his fares would be going that worried Galloway, it was that he and Minden had to gain time, which they could only do providing they made the police earn every inch of the trail by slow interrogations.

Minden subsided, watched the countryside whip past the window as they shot up, and over, and down the far side of the pass leading out of Los Angeles proper and over into the bedroom of the city, called San Fernando Valley. From there, the cab sped northwest towards the second, more distant pass that led from San Fernando Valley over into Simi Valley, which was a more distant, and more rural, city environ.

Galloway, with time to relax and think, took full advantage of the respite to evolve his theory of escape. He did not tell John Minden that he intended to jettison him, but as a matter of fact he knew perfectly well that as long as

Minden was with him, their chances of escaping at least police apprehension were very slight. His intention was to get Minden out of the city and well away, but he had never promised to do any more, and in fact he had not quite promised to do even that much.

When they were descending into Simi Valley over the Chatworth Pass, and night-time became more solidly dark because the rural countryside they were driving into had no roadside lights, Galloway thought he knew how he was going to leave the United States. He had several alternatives but the one that intrigued him the most was the one he knew Minden would find the least appealing. It was also the same option he felt reasonably certain Bennison and the police would also find the least appealing.

Their driver entered the lighted rural Simi Valley Airport, drew his hack to a halt out front of the lighted terminal building, and got out of his cab before either of his fares did. When Galloway alighted the driver had his hand out. Minden was annoyed but Galloway paid the fare and handed the driver a fair tip. All that veneer of cynical indifference melted and the driver smiled.

'Good luck,' he said to Galloway. 'Sir.'

They waited until the cab was making a big U-turn and heading back the way it had come, then entered the lighted airport building, found a clerk who was half asleep, roused him, discovered that there was a charter aircraft waiting on the line, and bought passage on it to Portland, Oregon. The clerk was so pleased — and probably so non-plussed — that he didn't even wait until Galloway and Minden were out of earshot before he picked up his intercommunication device, called for someone named 'Sharkey,' and said, 'Get warmed up and wide awake, you've got a pair of pigeons for Portland.'

Galloway saw Minden's look of distaste, smiled, lit a cigarette and said, 'In case you're hungry, there is a coffee machine, and next to it a candy machine.'

Minden wasn't hungry. He looked nervously at his watch, looked just as nervously out the large glass window where someone started an airplane engine, and shook his head at Galloway.

'I'm having misgivings. I'm not an enthusiastic flyer even on those big trans-oceanic aircraft. That thing out there sounds like an asthmatic swan.'

Galloway, with many hours of flight behind him, and the confidence of a man who had never thought he might be involved in an aircraft accident, went to the window, looked out, looked again, and touched Minden, then pointed. 'You seem to always have a choice. Do you see that black-and-white car cruising across the field?'

Minden looked, then stepped swiftly away from the window. 'They couldn't possibly be looking for us. How could the police know we are here?'

Galloway had an easy answer to that. 'If our hack-driver had any suspicions it wouldn't take him five minutes to telephone the local police, would it?'

Minden leaned and peeked around until he could see that cruising police car. It was inside the airport fence, but it seemed to be disinclined to hasten over to the building. In fact, as Minden and Galloway watched, the cruiser went easterly along the high fence, travelling at a very slow rate of speed, and flicking a searchlight up and down the wire. Evidently someone had reported a break in the high fence, which was community property, and the night-patrol had drawn the assignment to find the break.

Minden was enormously relieved. So was Galloway, although his apprehension had never been quite as bad as had Minden's.

A lean, gum-chewing young man came in, looked enquiringly around, and when the silent desk-clerk pointed to Galloway and Minden the gum-chewer strolled over and said, 'I'm ready any time you are. No luggage?'

Galloway shook his head. 'We're not going to be up there that long. Lead off, please.'

The pilot took them out into the cooling gloom and across to his twin-engine aircraft. As Minden climbed in first he made an unmistakable groan. The gum-chewing pilot looked up enquiringly.

Galloway paused it off with an apologetic small smile.

'My friend is not a very brave flyer. But he'll be all right once we're airborne.' Galloway stepped up, ducked down and got inside. There were places for four seated passengers, and the aircraft vibrated noticeably. Minden had some justification on his side; even Galloway did not feel greatly buoyed up when their pilot secured the doors, flicked on his running-lights, revved up the engines and called to someone over his intercom saying, 'Okay, Mutton-Head, keep the beer cold I'll be back for breakfast,' and with that unprofessional notification of departure, the aircraft's engines rose to a whine, and the vibrations increased until even Galloway had misgivings, then the pilot released his wheel-brakes and with a squeal of rubber they lunged and lurched ahead down the poorly-lighted runway. Minden was as white as a sheet.

17

Flight by Night

Portland, Oregon, was a large, bustling city with a port that entertained ships from Canada and the Orient, and with an industrial area that compared favourably as far as grime and smoke and dirt were concerned, with the industrial area of Los Angeles, or just about any other large city.

Portland also had a hilltop residential community where people of substance had their elegant and expensive homes, usually with at least one entire wall made of glass in order to overlook the city, the majestic river, and farther away, the white-capped high mountains.

Even when travellers arrived after midnight, there was still enough life stirring in the big city to keep strangers from being sources of much curiosity, although the hotel clerk where Galloway and Minden checked in raised his eyebrows over the lack of luggage. Galloway thought he had assuaged the clerk's disapproval when he said they had left their kits at the airport because they would be leaving early in the morning.

After being assigned a room, though, Galloway, who was finally hungry, dragged Minden, who had not come through the rough flight too well, back out into the chilly, breezy night in search of a restaurant. They found one not very distant from the hotel and Galloway ate like a horse while Minden, coming out of shock slowly, only sipped black tea.

To try and cheer Minden up, Galloway said, 'The lad who flew us up here intends to spend the night in Portland and not fly back until morning.'

Minden rolled his eyes. 'I shouldn't wonder. It ought to take even longer, for him to get his nerve up to do that over again.'

Galloway smiled, waited until the waiter had put down his meal and had departed, then said, 'Minden, the idea is that the pilot won't be back in Simi Valley tonight, in case the Los Angeles police get around to expanding their manhunt to the village airfields. That also means, if the pilot is going to sleep here, we don't have very much to worry about.'

Minden sipped his strong tea and looked baleful. 'Of course we've got plenty to worry about,' he grumbled, in contradiction. 'We're in Portland, Oregon, not Caracas, Venezuela, not Tunisia or Morocco.'

There was no point in carrying on this conversation. Minden did not want to be re-assured, he wanted to go right on savouring his fright and his gloominess. Galloway ate, enjoyed the meal, called for a cigar afterwards and when Minden wrinkled his nose Galloway laughed at him.

'This may be my last masculine fling, Minden, so I'm going to enjoy it.' Galloway arose, dropped a note atop the table and said, 'Let's get back to the hotel. I need some sleep, whether you do or not.'

It was late by the time Galloway showered and got to bed. Minden, in an adjoining bed, said he was still so tight-wound from that harrowing flight over the mountains in that vibrating little airplane that he probably would not be able to sleep all night long.

Galloway, with his revolver and his money in the bed with him, sighed with resignation. He did not expect Minden to do anything ridiculous, because by now Minden was entirely dependent upon him, but this close to making his last bid, Galloway chose not to take even any small chances, if he could avoid them, so he lay in the darkness staring at the ceiling, prepared to remain awake at least as long as Minden did.

The fate that takes care of such things must have touched Minden with her wand, because five minutes after the room was dark, Galloway heard his companion snoring. He smiled to himself in the darkness; for a man whose nerves were completely and perhaps even permanently frazzled, John Minden had made a really miraculous recovery.

When Galloway awakened the following morning Minden was already showering. There was a barber shop on the mezzanine floor and with beard-stubble to remind him that he badly needed a shave, when

Minden came forth freshly attired, Galloway suggested a visit to the barber before breakfast. Minden was agreeable. The only expression he showed this morning was one of dubious interest, as though, while expecting the worst, he was hoping for the best.

There was one barber in the shop on the mezzanine floor when they got down there. There were four chairs, but as the barber said, it was a bit early; in fact, ordinarily that one barber did not arrive for another half to three-quarters of an hour.

Minden got the first shave. As Galloway waited he went out to look at the lobby and dining-room by broad daylight. The hotel had not been very impressive the previous night, but then under the circumstances surrounding their arrival last night, nothing had looked very impressive.

By daylight, though, the hotel was clean and sunbright and well-kept-looking. It was too early for the lobby to be very full, but the dining-room was beginning to fill up, and that pleased Galloway who had developed an affinity for crowds, just since the previous night. He had also developed an affinity for aircraft flights, so while he killed time awaiting his turn in the barber's chair, he telephoned out to the Portland International Airport and reserved one seat on the Pan-American flight going over the polar route across the Atlantic to London. He also reserved a seat for one passenger on the twelve o'clock flight to Caracas, Venezuela, by way of Mexico City and Puerta Vallarta.

Then he went back see if the barber had finished with Minden, discovered that he had, and sent Minden on along to get them a table in the dining-room while Galloway got his shave.

It felt exceptionally good to have a hot towel on his face, to be shaved by an expert, and not to be bored to distraction with the customary locquaciousness of barbers. In fact, although Galloway had only recently arisen from a long sleep, he could have gone to sleep again in the barber's chair. The main reason he didn't was because, before joining Minden in the dining-room, he had several errands to run, and he had to run them without making his absence look needlessly long.

By the time he got to the table, a little breathless because some of Galloway's purchases hadn't been available in the hotel's shops, Minden was half through his breakfast. He looked up, watched Galloway take a seat, then cocked his head and said, 'You weren't all this time just getting shaved, were you?'

A waiter came and Galloway ordered before he answered. He was as hungry this morning as he had been last night, as though hunger were a cumulative thing. Neither he nor Minden had eaten much the day before, they had been too tense and guyed-up to be hungry, but this was another day, a long way from the seat of their troubles, and it seemed easier to relax and be hungry.

When Galloway looked around the room, which was full now, and mutedly noisy with the bright breakfast talk of the hotel's guests, he said, 'I had some things to buy and leave in the room upstairs. Also, I made a reservation for you on the noon flight to Venezuela.'

Minden's fork stopped in mid-air, then very slowly descended. 'Venezuela? Is that where we're going?'

'No. That's where *you* are going. I'll give you the name you'll use to pick up the ticket right after we've gone upstairs and changed our clothes.'

'But why Venezuela? I think the United States has an extradition treaty with them down there.'

Galloway's eggs and toast and coffee arrived. 'Because,' he explained to John Minden, 'you mentioned it as though it were desirable, and as for extradition treaties, I can tell you candidly that about the only countries that do not have treaties with the United States, Britain, West Germany, France, and the other democracies, are the Red-bloc nations, and do you have any idea what they do to decadent imperialists who arrive in their countries seeking asylum — with a fat moneybelt wrapped round their middle?'

Minden ate no more but he lit a cigarette to accompany his tea, and sat gazing with an almost clinical detachment at Galloway. Finally, he said, 'Well; as a matter of fact I have friends in Caracas, so if I make it down there I'll be all right. Do you mind telling me where you are going?'

Galloway smiled. 'Yes, I mind.' He went on eating his breakfast, which was both tasty and adequate, although the coffee was too strong.

Minden took the rebuff well, and changed the subject. It was quite possible that Minden did not really care very much where Galloway might be going. Minden's concern was for Minden's welfare. But he had another nagging thought, which he mentioned now.

'What possible assurance do either of us have that we'll reach our destinations?'

Galloway was slightly laconic about that. 'Probably about as good an assurance as anyone could have under these circumstances, plus an idea a man I know in London gave me some time back, with elaborations that even he probably would not care to claim.'

Minden said, 'Fine. Whatever all that means. But you've done well so far.' There was something else troubling

Minden, and it probably had been bothering him for some time. 'It occurs to me, Mister Whatever-your-name-is, that you are the only one in all this who is coming out smelling roses. You've made us all look rather bad, including Bennison and the police. The odd part is that you really don't have the proper image for some kind of international Raffles-type.' Minden put out his cigarette. 'You are coming out of this a rich man, aren't you?'

Galloway raised his eyes, saw Minden's envious expression, and said, 'Just to ease your jealousy, I'll tell you that all I'm getting out of this is the money.'

'And the paintings,' said Minden, smiling acidly. 'You wouldn't want to forget them, would you?'

'I'm not forgetting them, Minden, and they won't fetch me a red cent.' Galloway looked one last time around the noisy, busy dining-room, then saw Minden's stare, and said, 'Not one healthy copper. Now, if you've finished there, suppose we go upstairs and get ready to drive to the airport.'

Minden leaned on the table but not to arise, to speak. 'Listen; before you do something quixotic about those paintings, let me make you a proposition. I'll give you the address of some friends in Venezuela where you can send them, and I'll pay you one hundred thousand dollars upon receipt.'

Galloway almost laughed. Minden, the art dealer, despite all he had lost, and all he had most recently been through to avoid being punished for his crookedness, was still inherently the crooked art dealer.

Galloway started to arise. 'Minden, you couldn't buy them. And let me pass on one word of advice to you. If you insist on remaining in your no-doubt lucrative crooked art business, don't ever touch those six paintings again, because the next time it won't be someone averse to killing you that'll be dropping round. Okay?'

Galloway arose and stood waiting for his companion. As they threaded their way through the room and on across the lobby towards the row of lifts, John Minden, morose-looking and thoughtful, paced beside Galloway without saying a word. Galloway's warning had evidently rather well soaked in.

Upstairs in the corridor outside their room two men who had the well-fed, slightly flashy look of travelling salesmen, were standing across the hall in earnest conversation. They looked up and nodded at Galloway and Minden, then resumed their discussion as Galloway opened the door to the opposite room and led the way in. A moment later, when Minden was gazing with some surprise at the packages on the chairs and sofa of their room, Galloway leaned and listened at the door.

Those salesmen-types were still talking out there. As near as Galloway could make out, they were comparing impressions of some local buyer who had a terrific amount of sales resistance. It all seemed genuine enough, but according to Morton Galloway's calculations, the next two hours would be the most critical; if one could assume that by now the Los Angeles police had shown pictures, or at least pen-and-ink drawings that were supposedly likenesses, of Galloway and

Minden, to those people out at the rural Santa Susanna airport in Simi valley, the Portland police teletypes would undoubtedly be clattering their little mechanical heads off.

As Galloway straightened around from his listening posture at the door, Minden had looked into a brown paper bag, and was now standing there, shocked to the eyes, making a bleating kind of a question.

'What in the name of God is this; are you crazy?'

Galloway would have laughed at another time. Now, he not only didn't laugh, he told Minden to start shedding his clothes.

18

A Matter of Cold Legs

It took longest to shave their legs, otherwise, excepting for John Minden's constant high-pitched bleating, the actual transformation was a lot less difficult than Galloway had thought it might be, considering the fact that although he had been shrewd in his purchases, he had never before in his life done anything like this.

Minden's discomfort was understandable, especially when he adjusted the padded brassière at the dressing-table mirror, and got into the panty-hose, while Galloway grinned from across the room where he was adjusting some shoulder-straps. Minden reached for the very smart knitted skirt and glared.

'Just exactly how do we pass this off if we're caught!'

According to Galloway, that was the

whole idea of the disguise: *Not* to get caught. He pointed to the safety razor and make-up kit. 'Shave your eyebrows until they'll pass, and when you put that hat on make certain some of your hair is pulled low and swept up over your ears. And Minden, when you stand, don't hold your legs wide apart, and when you sit down, cross them.'

Minden made a bleak and unflattering comment concerning men who masqueraded as women, but he got into the knit two-piece suit and stood looking at himself in the mirror with an expression of grudging disbelief. Then he went over where the razor and makeup kit were, and said over his shoulder he thought Galloway could have come up with something better than this.

Galloway did not defend himself. He had never in his life had anything constrict his movement as that skirt did. Minden's remarks went entirely unheeded while he concentrated on what he had to do, and what he had to learn, such as how women walk in tight shoes and those constricting skirts.

Minden came away from the make-up kit and razor looking surprisingly feminine. He put on the little pert hat, arranged his hair, looked long at himself in the dressing-table mirror, and finally went to put his suit into one of the suitcases on the sofa while he waited for Galloway to finish his disguise. He said, 'If this works I'll still never feel like telling anyone.'

Galloway understood the feeling. 'If it works,' he said, 'you'll probably have to fight off the amorous lads on the Caracas flight who traditionally make passes at American women.'

Minden had a blistering comment about that, snapped closed the suitcase and looked at his wristwatch. 'One hour to wait,' he said, in a low grumble, and went over to a window to look outward and downward.

Galloway gave him two orders. 'Minden, telephone down for a cab to be waiting — and take that damned man's wristwatch off!'

For Galloway, the idea of a female disguise had come as the result of some brain-racking to discover some method by which two male fugitives might be able to board an international aircraft. It was improbable that the Los Angeles police would be able to put a plainclothes man on every airplane leaving the West Coast from Los Angeles to Seattle, up in Washington state, and it was improbable that the Los Angeles police would really believe their fugitives might even have got out of Los Angeles yet, because they would also have had surveillance teams at all the orthodox air terminals waiting to nab the men whose descriptions and likenesses they undoubtedly had. But that certainly did not preclude sending out teletypes to every other city police department all the way from Seattle down to San Diego, and perhaps even inland just in case the fugitives did actually manage to get out of the city, perhaps in theory by car.

Of course there was no reason for the Los Angeles police to be positive the fugitives would try to flee the country, unless of course they knew enough about Galloway to think that, as an Englishman, he might try to get back overseas. But even then, it was also possible that the police might decide to concentrate on their citywide dragnet, on the basis that the fugitives, thinking the airports would be thoroughly covered, would attempt to lie low and hide out in the city.

Any way Galloway looked at it, the risk was great. Once he and Minden walked into the Portland airport building, even though they split up, and even though their disguises were actually quite good, they would be taking the final step and even when they were airborne, they would be trapped with no possible escape route left open, if the authorities on the ground found out who they were and flashed the message aloft.

For them both, there was one bad flaw. Minden did not think of it until Galloway, finally dressed and ready to leave the room, said, 'You'd better be a fast talker, Minden. I have no idea how the Venezuelans are about people arriving in their country without passports, but where I'm going they are very stuffy about things like that.'

Minden, near the door, turned very slowly and stared. 'That's great. How do we get around it?'

Galloway already had the answer as to how *he* would get around it. His passport, the same one he'd used to leave England and to arrive in the United States, was tucked away in the inside jacket pocket of his masculine attire in the suitcase he was carrying. He anticipated changing back shortly before arriving at London airport, but if that proved impossible he was reconciled to being taken into custody by the immigration authorities, and having Inspector Merritt come down and alibi him out. It would actually serve Merritt right if he had to do that, and humiliate himself in the process by having to plead for a man dressed as a woman. There was a name for men with that bizarre addiction.

As to how John Minden would manage, once he was face to face with Venezuelan immigration people, Galloway had no idea. Neither did he have much concern. He went to the door, opened it, motioned for Minden to precede him, and when he afterwards closed the door he said, 'You're going to have to stop thinking in terms of 'we', Mister Minden. From the moment we walk into the airport building I'm going one way and you are to go another way. Your flight reservation is in the name of Harriet Stowe. S-t-o-w-e.' Galloway closed the door and preceded Minden to the lift, punched the button, looked Minden up and down, and had to smile. John Minden actually made a very attractive woman. He looked a little hard and just a hint past the first blush of youth, but not so far past men would not turn for a second look. Galloway said, 'Were you aware that Latins make lousy lovers?'

Minden grimaced and stepped into the lift when it arrived clutching his suitcase as though it were a weapon. 'I dread walking across the damned lobby,' he muttered, and proved it when they arrived downstairs by hanging back until Galloway was out of the lift and had to look back with a frown. Minden fixed his eyes upon the doors beyond and marched beside Galloway all the way across the lobby where several men looked him up and down. When they reached the pavement beyond where a cab-driver was lounging against his hack, Minden, red in the face, said, 'You and your insane ideas!'

The cab-driver also looked Minden up and down as he held the door for his fares, and afterwards when he leaned down he offered Minden an almost greasy-sweet smile when he asked their destination. Galloway said, 'The airport,' and as the fat, smiling face withdrew, Galloway looked around and kept a perfectly straight face as he saw the high colour and the angry eyes of his companion. Another time this situation might have been hilarious.

Galloway noticed two things on the ride to the airport. One; his legs were cold. Two; the driver spent about as much time looking in his rearview mirror as he did looking at the road ahead.

At the airport when Galloway paid the driver, he turned and gave John Minden another of those unctiously greasy-sweet smiles. Minden picked up the suitcase, turned and indignantly hitched at his skirt as he struck out for the main entrance to the airport building.

Portland International Airport was in some ways more sophisticated and worldly than the Los Angeles terminal; at Portland nearly all incoming West Coast flights from the Orient, from Japan, Hong Kong, the Philippines, and the hundreds of in-between places in the Pacific community of nations, landed first. There was a very busy immigration facility at Portland airport, and the upstairs lounge was not only crowded and noisy, it was also teeming with people of a dozen racial and ethnic affinities.

Galloway met Minden just inside the main doors. Minden had been waiting. He stepped over to an alcoved window where some horseshoe-shaped upholstered benches were, and said, 'I don't think this is so smart, splitting up just yet.'

Galloway thought that remark did not come from any reasoned response, but came instead from Minden's fear of terminating his association with the man who had thus far managed to keep them both free and alive. As far as Galloway was concerned, he had done everything he'd said he would do, and a bit more. He gave Minden a stony stare and pointed towards the ticket-counter across the busy foyer.

'You are Harriet Stowe. If they don't detect you on the airplane, you'll have plenty of time to figure out a way to get around the Venezuelan immigration people. Maybe your friends down there can help. But as of this minute, Harriet, you sure as hell are on your own.' Galloway dropped his arm with an indication of finality. He and John Minden looked at one another, then the fugitive art dealer said, 'Okay. But I don't believe I owe you any thanks.'

Galloway's lips curled. He picked up the suitcase he had previously set down, turned on his heel and strode away without looking back. As far as he was concerned, that was the end of an in-advertent and enforced acquaintanceship. He was perfectly glad to see it end, too, as he strode alone over to pick up the ticket reserved in the name of Mary Louise Merritt.

Galloway's flight would leave an hour before Minden's South American flight. When Galloway had checked in his baggage he went out to the upstairs flight deck and had a smoke, stole a peek at his masculine wristwatch, which was in a suit pocket, and stamped his feet because his legs were still cold. He marvelled that women could go around like this all year round and not suffer as he was suffering.

He saw enormous jets arrive and take off, saw smaller, inland and coastwise aircraft, usually of the propeller-variety, land and leave on different runways. Portland airport was a very busy place.

Finally, he saw the parade of foreign aircraft that were lined up after being emptied of passengers, awaiting either re-fuelling or the time for their re-scheduling, and among them were several airliners from South and Central America. It probably would have been possible to secure a seat for Minden on one of those airliners; Galloway had had no way of knowing, and it probably was of no great importance anyway.

He finished his smoke, preferred to

avoid the main lounge just in case Minden was having a case of nerves, and went along one of the long ramps below the upper deck to where it was possible, by making out numbers on the aircraft being serviced in the flight line, to determine which would be his.

While he was standing in front of a huge window watching, he saw a shiny, dark car cruise in from the main entrance. There were other cars, and cabs, but this particular car struck Galloway for no reason that he could define right at the moment, as being a police vehicle. He watched it all the way up to the front approach, and there he had to move across the room to another window to see it park in a place where the red kerbing plus the large No Parking sign would have discouraged just about any driver except a policeman, and there he watched as two large men in plain business suits alighted and headed for the main foyer.

Galloway's opinion was equally divided between the probability that this was some kind of routine police call, and the probability that those two plainclothes men were looking for a pair of men who had flown into Portland from Simi Valley the previous night.

He left the place of vantage and went back down the long ramp towards the main foyer, but instead of entering it he went outside by a side door, walked to the nearest front window out where the cab stand was, and looked in. He did not see the pair of unobtrusive large men right away. Neither did he see Minden, which was a relief. But eventually he saw the pair of detectives come together over in front of the Pan-American flight counter as though they had already visited another counter or two, and this time, when they moved up to the counter, they showed the clerk two photographs, at least from where Galloway was watching, they looked like photographs, and his heart sank as the clerk studied them, then shook his head and turned to call up another clerk.

19

In the High Sky

When the loudspeaker announced that Galloway's flight was ready to receive passengers and gave the gate number, Galloway went inside the main foyer looking for Minden. It was his intention to explain about the pair of detectives. He did not find Minden, but neither was his search either very prolonged or very zealous. He abandoned it, finally, with a perfectly clear conscience, and went out to board his own flight. He did not see either of those plainclothes men although he looked for them, and was a little relieved when he left the building to go up the ramp into the aircraft.

One of the detectives was standing at the juncture of the loading-ramp and entrance to the airplane. He was looking at every passenger, as they moved past him at less than three feet and stepped inside the aircraft. Galloway should have had a temporary stoppage of the heart, but for some inexplicable reason he swung past the detective without giving the man more than a glance. It did not really hit Galloway until he was taking his seat in the airplane that he was now, finally and irrevocably, cornered. Before, and up to the moment he sat in the airplane, there had been room to manoeuvre in. Now, he was confined as surely as though he were in a cell. It was a distinctly unpleasant sensation, but in another sense, the fact that he had been able to reach the airplane, to take a seat, meant that he was finally on the last leg of his adventure. The most perilous, in one way, but at least the final, leg of it.

The aircraft filled slowly. A thickly-made youngish man with a military haircut stood near the main aisle as people trouped in, and studied each one individually. It did not dawn on Galloway, who assumed this was another policeman, that the youngish man was in fact one of the armed guards most American airplanes had on board to detect and prevent air piracy, if they could. The youngish man did not look especially formidable, and there was certainly no sign of a weapon. Galloway, who had put his own gun under the mattress of the hotel bed back in the city, and who had felt immeasurably relieved the moment he got rid of the thing, wondered if it were even remotely possible that his polar flight might have a skyjacker on board. It was a preposterous thought; aircraft bound for London were about as far off the track for hi-jackings to Cuba, which was where most air pirates diverted their airplanes, or so Galloway reassuringly told himself, as an aircraft could be.

The loading was eventually completed, a small lighted sign suggested that all seat-straps be adjusted into place, and the steady climb of the wind-up sounds from the motor nacelles sounded much louder outside than they sounded inside, but in either case anyone who knew the meaning, understood from those sounds that the airplane had been cleared and would shortly now start its ungainly crawl

238

out to the flight line for the take-off.

Galloway lit a cigarette, and at once was tapped on the shoulder by a smiling stewardess. He had forgotten, and promptly put out the smoke. No smoking was allowed during take-offs or landings. He was annoyed with himself, not because of the cigarette but because by lighting it, and having to be told to put it out, he had drawn attention to himself. That was the one thing Galloway did not want to do.

He felt the aircraft begin to move, and leaned to crane out the nearest porthole for a quick, and limited, look for either of those plainclothes men, or for their shiny car when the aircraft finally waddled around where it was possible to see the front of the building. The car was still there, and that meant the detectives were still conducting their search. Galloway eased back with a false sense of security, told himself the aircraft could be stopped any minute, and that even after it was airborne it could be diverted to a local landing field, and he still felt as though he were escaping in spite of all his own logic. There had to be some explanation for this sensation but Galloway did not bother seeking it.

The airplane stopped waddling with its nose tipped up and its tail tipped down. The motors died, then began a steady strong surge. The airplane vibrated, Galloway looked towards the distant airport passenger building, hoped Minden would make it simply because if Minden *didn't* make it there was a most excellent possibility that his admissions would make sure Galloway didn't make it either, and that was the moment the airplane began its long run down the take-off strip, picking up speed and vibrating terribly right up to the moment before lift-off, then everything except the high-pitched whine seemed to fade out. The next moment Galloway was shoved hard back into his seat, the airplane fought for altitude, and behind it a streamer of black exhaust made a plume across the lower sky.

A fat man across the aisle from Galloway flicked loose his safety belt before the light went off, before anyone else removed their belts, and drew out a racing form and a pencil and became wholly immersed in some endeavour that was uniquely his own.

Finally, as the pert little stewardess passed in the aisle, she nodded and winked at Galloway. The No Smoking sign was no longer lighted. But Galloway was out of the niton for the time being, so he merely nodded back.

The youngish man up front was still seated facing back towards the interior of the passenger's segment of the airliner. To Galloway it seemed a little melodramatic to have this armed guard, or whatever he was, sitting up there arms crossed over his chest, like some oldtime shotgun-courier or whatever they were called, who rode the oldtime Western stagecoaches, keeping an eye peeled for highwaymen, Indians, ambushes, or whatever.

Galloway lost interest eventually and had a smoke. He also had a highball when the stewardess came along with her little cart. He had somewhere between seven and nine hours of this ahead of him. The most objectionable part about trans-atlantic flights was the sitting; the everlasting, monumentally boring, sitting.

There was a television screen mounted just over the doorway up ahead, and there were earphones for people wishing to hear endless hours of tinned music. There was also reading, and that, Galloway noticed, seemed most popular on this particular flight, but for he, himself, it was the enforced physical inactivity that palled.

After a couple of hours he settled the seat back, arranged himself as comfortably as he could for sleep, and closed his eyes. Immediately the stewardess came to offer him his dinner. He had to re-adjust the seat and act grateful for a meal he felt absolutely no desire for, and he had to do it all without opening his mouth. In every way that was visibly obvious, Galloway could pass as a woman, but not vocally, and that had been a cause for some anxiety from the first moment they had left the hotel. Now, in the constriction of the airplane where he knew from long experience how easy it was to strike up friendships, Galloway had to be particularly careful. He had thought it might be possible to discourage conversations by pretending to sleep or drowse most of the way across the roof of the world, and actually, after that highball he probably could have slept for several hours, except that his dinner arrived.

He toyed with the food and patiently awaited until the tray was taken away, then he eased the seat back to try again. This time he was more fortunate. Except for a man somewhere close by smoking a vile cigar, Galloway was left untroubled, but instead of sleeping his mind jumped from the grim face of Howard Bennison as he imagined it looked by now, to an imagined scene where John Minden was discovered to be a man masquerading as a woman on his Caracas flight, and breaking down and telling the police all about Galloway also flying out of Portland airport.

He even had visions of that package he had mailed to Inspector Merritt getting lost. Of course, if that happened, Galloway might just as well re-embark the moment he touched down at Heathrow, and fly somewhere else — *anywhere* else — because he would never be able to convince Inspector Merritt he had not decided to re-steal the paintings and sell them, perhaps on the Continent. He had even made some such remark to Merritt before leaving for the States.

Of all the unpleasant thoughts he had, and of all the faces he saw against the inside of his closed eyelids, he thought, one particular face and statement stood out: Inspector Merritt the morning he had sat in Galloway's flat in London saying, 'One last time,' as though Galloway were some great sporting figure being urged to defend a championship for some vague, final triumph.

One last time could mean anything, actually, and if Galloway had interpreted it to be a kind of oblique accolade, coming as it had from a policeman of Merritt's stature, maybe it was his vanity that had landed him in the mess he was just now beginning to extricate himself from; maybe Merritt hadn't meant it as Galloway had taken it at all.

There was one consolation: If Galloway pulled this off and made it home free, he could adopt those three words as a kind of personal motto, meaning that this was, indeed, the last time for him. He was getting too old to enjoy the strain and he had enough money anyway. Some men lived dangerously because excitement became a kind of narcotic to them. This was not so with Galloway, and that may have been why he had been successful in the past; his pragmatism was based upon practicality and hard facts, nothing less.

The airplane got a little buffeting and Galloway opened his eyes just as the voice of one of the officers up front announced over the intercommunication system that they were encountering high winds over the Atlantic, but were going up a little higher and would soon elude them. The gross man across the aisle saw Galloway's eyes open and said, 'That ain't ordinary wind, lady, that's the backrap from the Angel Gabriel's trumpet.' He smiled, evidently wishing to be reassuring. 'On my last crossing it was about this time that we began to run low on fuel because we were overloaded, and had to land at some lousy military base in Newfoundland. You'd have thought we was a 'plane load of Communist spies the way they herded us into a big room and wouldn't let us leave it until the damned airplane was refuelled, then they herded us back aboard so we wouldn't see anything. What in hell kind of secret stuff could they have in an icebox like Newfoundland, anyway?' The gross man shook his head and glanced at a gold wristwatch. 'Go on back to sleep, lady, from here on there's nothing but boredom with a capital B.'

Galloway turned his head away and closed his eyes again. The fat man was one of those harmless, rather garrulous passengers who were actually the least objectionable of all the various types one met on overseas flights.

Sleep never did quite come to Galloway, although he drowsed for an hour or more before giving up and swinging the seat back upright into a sitting position again, and lighting a cigarette. The stewardess came round to ask who would care for a highball. A few people were willing, but mostly, this being a kind of grey period, the young woman got only unsmiling head-shakes. Galloway, who was not really much of a hard-liquor drinker anyway, declined and began reading one of the coloured folders contained in the pouch on the back of the seat in front of him. It was all about the Bahamas, and Galloway was positive they were exactly as heavenly as the pictures and text implied, but he had no more desire to see the Bahamas right at that moment, then he had to see Cannes or Nice, two places he had visited often and had usually liked. All he wanted to see now was London airport, and after that his flat — and his regular attire again.

The gross man across the aisle began to furiously rummage all his pockets, and after a moment he leaned and said, 'Lady; could I bum a cigarette off you?'

Galloway dug out his pack and held it out. The man reached to take a cigarette, and Galloway saw his eyes slowly widen as he looked steadily at the strong hand holding out the packet. Galloway shoved the pack closer and as soon as the gross man had taken a cigarette, withdrew both hand and pack.

The gross man lit up, said, 'Thank

you,' and did not even turn his head towards Galloway again, as he leaned back in his seat and unblinkingly studied the ceiling as he smoked, and faintly frowned.

Galloway's lifelong idea that anyone stepping out of his proper environment, was bound to make at the very least one bad mistake, was borne out once again. He should have remembered to also buy women's gloves when he'd been buying all that other stuff.

He kept a wary eye on the gross man, but even after that individual had finished his smoke, he continued to sit over there relaxed and thoughtful, and quiet. Whatever he thought he knew about Galloway, or had guessed, did not really matter as long as he kept it to himself at least until they reached London, and Galloway had a chance to disappear in the crowds.

20

Aloft and Alert

Galloway speculated, when he was sure half the flight was behind them, that regardless of what happened now, he would not be returned to an American airfield, and thus to U.S. jurisdiction, and that made him loosen a little.

They would not turn his flight around even if they thought they had a much-wanted international felon aboard, when it was about equal distance to London as to the nearest U.S. airfield. If the police were waiting at London airport, Galloway felt more confident of regaining his freedom than if he had been taken by American police. At least in London he knew one man to call if he needed help. Of course it was possible that Merritt might not help him, but he thought that possibility was really rather remote for the basic reason that if Merritt refused to help him, and if he chose to explain what he had been up to, and why he had undertaken the assignment in the first place, Inspector Merritt's name would inevitably come up.

As for Merritt denying anything, that would be difficult to do when the returned paintings showed up in his possession.

Galloway felt reasonably secure. Not safe, exactly, because while he was sitting perfectly motionless thirty thousand or so feet over the dark Atlantic, back on the American mainland there was bound to be a lot of energetic activity in progress, but at least he was still moving, still employing evasive tactics, and for the Americans time was running out. Even if he were apprehended at London airport, there would be the ensuing complicated business of extraditing him back to the States, and actually he really was not that important a criminal.

He could only guess what the Americans might charge him with — car theft, flight to avoid prosecution, some other lesser illegalities, possibly even breaking and entering, for his witnessed-burglary of Bennison's residence, but he did not view any of those charges as serious enough to warrant the time and expense of an official extradition.

But there was one other consideration: Mitreman's murder. If the American police thought Galloway was in any way connected with that, he could be considered a very worthwhile felon. A man did not have to actually pull a trigger and kill someone; if it could be proved he knew the murder was to be committed, or if it could be proved he was in any way connected with a murder, he was equally as liable under American law as the actual murderer. *That* might make Galloway a worthwhile suspect to the Americans.

The stewardess came down the aisle looking at each passenger. When she saw Galloway was wide awake she smilingly offered to get 'her' a sleeping pill and a glass of water. Galloway smiled and shook 'her' head. The stewardess turned to the gross man with the same offer. He seemed to have trouble deciding, then he slowly nodded at the girl, and as she moved off down the rearward aisle, the gross man took his limp racing form from an inside pocket, took a gold pen from the same pocket, and wrote furiously in a cramped hand on the naked margin. As he secretively tore this written segment from the racing sheet, being careful to do this surreptitiously, the fat man then balled up the note in one hand while he returned the racing form to his inside pocket with the other hand.

Galloway dug out his cigarettes, lit one, looked stonily at the gross man, and held out the packet. As the fat man turned his head Galloway leaned and smiled at him. 'Put the note in my hand,' he said, making no attempt to disguise his voice. 'Take a cigarette, and put the note in my hand!'

The fat man paled and hesitated to pluck a cigarette from the packet, but eventually, when he did so, he reluctantly dropped the balled up bit of paper into Galloway's hand. Then he pulled away, lit his cigarette with an unsteady hand, and sat across the aisle staring straight ahead at the yonder bulkhead over the close-cropped hairdo of the armed guard who

252

was sitting up there sipping coffee and looking tired, or bored, or perhaps a little of both.

The pert little stewardess returned with a paper cup of water and a small white pill. Galloway stared at the fat man willing him to take the pill. The fat man really had no choice since he had asked for it, and since the girl had brought it to him, so he accepted it, thanked the girl and held the pill in one hand, the paper cup in the other hand, until the girl went forward, and he probably would not have taken the pill if Galloway had not been malevolently staring at him.

With a sigh, the gross man downed the pill, swallowed the water, and resumed smoking as he settled back again. His attitude now was that of complete resignation, as though the relaxant were some kind of needed escape from a very awkward situation. While he sat like that Galloway unrolled the balled up paper and read the scribbled message: 'The lady across the aisle from me is really a man in disguise. Stewardess, you had better warn the guard. There may be a hijacking in the wind.'

Galloway pocketed the note, looked at the gross man, who was ignoring Galloway as hard as he could, and after a moment of contemplation, Galloway rummaged for a piece of paper and a pen to also write a note, but this one to be handed across the aisle, to the fat man.

'Mind your own business, have a nice flight, keep your damned mouth closed, and arrive in London refreshed and in one piece. There is to be no hijacking. There is to be no trouble at all, so don't try to make any.'

The gross man accepted the note and Galloway watched him read it. Afterwards, the fat man put out his cigarette, pocketed the balled up note from Galloway, turned up on to his side with his back to Galloway, and composed himself for sleep. Galloway watched, speculating about the pill the stranger had taken, decided it could not possibly be strong enough to induce lethargy this quickly, and almost decided that the fat man had decided to take Galloway's advice and mind his own business. The reason he did not quite accept that premise was because both the fat man's hands and arms were in front of him, hidden from Galloway's view by the man's whale-like big back.

He could have let it go, except that whatever the gross man was up to now meant trouble, and with something like four hours of flight left to live through, Galloway was not inclined, after all he had gone through, to be taken this near the end of the trail. Subconsciously, it also annoyed him that after out-witting a very successful American solicitor-racketeer, and the police too, he was now being imperilled by some fat salesman.

Galloway felt like arising, leaning over the fat man to see what he was doing with his hands in front of him, and giving him another warning. It was dark enough; the interior lights had been dimmed to facilitate sleeping, but there was a watchful stewardess up front talking to the youngish man with a military haircut. Perhaps, if Galloway had been dressed in his normal, masculine, attire, he could have done that, but if a woman stepped over to lean across a male passenger when the lights were low and most passengers were sleeping, when the stewardess and the guard knew those two people had not come aboard as a couple, it would stir up a lot more notoriety for Galloway than he could stand.

He decided on another note, wrote one, leaned to tap the fat man, and when that porcine face came around looking wary and wide awake, Galloway felt satisfied that his self-appointed adversary was up to something.

All Galloway's note said was for the fat man to lie on his back with both hands in plain sight.

Galloway waited. Eventually, like a porpoise heaving his bulk out of the water, the gross man rolled up on to his back in the seat and folded both hands upon his great belly. He looked at peace with the world but Galloway had no illusions; whoever the man was, whatever he did for a living, he was alert, observant, and perceptive. He may have been grossly overweight, and because of this in appearance sluggish, but Galloway knew differently. He even became a little curious about this enterprising adversary and sat there studying the man trying to guess something about him.

A half hour passed without the fat man moving, then he held out a hand across the aisle and growled one word: 'Cigarette.'

Galloway handed the man his entire packet, signalled the stewardess, handed her a note and asked her to bring him a fresh pack. The girl smiled and walked away, and the fat man turned his head, studied Galloway impassively, then fished out his racing sheet and pen again, writing a note in plain sight. When he finished he passed it across to Galloway, racing-sheet and all.

'You're a cornered rat,' Galloway read. 'They will get you at London airport. You are not armed. No one gets aboard without passing through the electronic weapons detector. I'm not armed either, but that young buck up front facing towards us is armed. All I've got to do is stand up and walk up there and tell him about you. Even if you make a scene, he's got the gun, you haven't.'

Galloway saw the stewardess returning with his cigarettes and waited until she had delivered them to write an answer to the fat man's note, right below it on the same racing form.

'I told you, there is to be no trouble, but if you want to make yourself a laughing stock, just try and make something sinister out of transvestitism. I harm no one, and this just happens to be my thing. There's no law against it; a lot of women dress like men.'

Galloway handed back the racing sheet and lit a cigarette without looking at the fat man for a long time. When he finally turned his head, the fat man was staring at Galloway with an expression of revulsion and fascination. Galloway didn't really blame him. Galloway would also have been just as intrigued by such a social aberration if he had encountered one. In fact, he would have felt the same degree of revulsion.

As things now stood, Galloway thought he had caused a stand-off. At least until they touched down in London. He could not really ask for, nor expect, anything better no matter what happened.

For a while the fat man lay over there, hands clasped, head tilted to the contour of the tipped-back seat, as motionless as anyone could be who was lost in thought, and while Galloway was encouraged, he also was wary. The fat man was undeniably very enterprising. When he looked the least harmful seemed to be when he was actually most dangerous. But Galloway had done all he could do until the fat man made another move.

He did not know exactly what he would do if the fat man made good his threat to arise and walk up where the armed guard was. Of course he could trip him, could perhaps cow him some way, but he could do nothing without drawing attention to himself, which would be just about as perilous as allowing the fat man to talk to the guard. He finally decided that if worst came to worst he would tell the armed guard the same story: That dressing as a woman was his thing. Aberrationists who were once a furtive minority, nowadays were no longer furtive at all, and even though most were still minorities, in the permissive society as long as they caused no trouble, people were inclined not to bother them.

Beyond the portholes there was a pale, sickly kind of greyish sky which made Galloway think they weren't more than perhaps an hour or an hour and a half from landing in London. His nerves tightened a bit as the end of the trail became dimly visible. He was irritated by that fat man, too. The police, and even the American underworld, had not been able to put a hand upon Galloway, and now he was threatened by some ham-and-egg salesman from the Kansas corn-belt.

The fat man turned, gazed at Galloway, then fished inside his outer jacket pocket and passed over a small leather folder. Inside was a large metal badge with the name R. J. Reynold across it, and below the name a number and one more word: Detective, and below that designation the legend: Chicago Police Department.

Galloway looked at the head-on photo-graph of the fat man which was in the folder, then closed the thing and handed it back, shrugged without speaking and shook his head as though none of this meant much to him. The fat man put up his identification folder, sighed, assumed a pained expression, and continued to gaze dead ahead. He was clearly a lot more qualified to cause Galloway trouble than Galloway had originally thought, even when they touched down in London. Also, the fat man was unlikely to be a novice at whatever he eventually decided to do.

Galloway's only hope seemed to be to stick to his contention that he was one of those aberrationists who dressed as a woman, and pray that the detective from Chicago decided that he would, indeed, look foolish, if he tried to make some kind of a case against Galloway for nothing more serious than that.

21

Good-Bye, Chicago Detective!

Very gradually, the sky seemed to brighten, although as a matter of fact it had never really turned completely black. The airplane had seemed to be chasing the dawn, had seemed always to be on the verge of over-taking daylight, and while the heavens were a corpse-like grey for some time, when the lights came up again there was a fresh-dawning kind of delightful pinkish glow beyond the portholes. Even Galloway felt his spirits respond to this fresh newness.

Across the aisle the fat man ran a hand over his beard-shadowed heavy features and when the stewardess came to sympathize because the sleeping pill hadn't worked, the fat man smiled at her and said it was nothing. That was the first time Galloway had seen the fat man smile; it clearly meant that whatever the fat man had decided to do about Galloway, was firmly fixed in his mind. He was no longer bothered by uncertainty. Galloway watched the man from the corner of his eye, and hoped.

As the passengers awakened there was some activity; a few people headed for the tail-section, some sat up looking around as though unable or unwilling to believe where they were, and a mumbling kind of garrulous growling became audible up and down the long aisle as couples straightened their seats, yawned, scratched, otherwise fidgetted, and eventually began to look anticipatory as the aroma of breakfast came up through the aisle.

The youngish man up front, facing the passengers, left his post and disappeared for'ard in the direction of the cockpit. The fat man suddenly heaved up to his feet, stretched, stepped across to the empty seat next to the window beside Galloway, and dropped down again. He did not look at Galloway as he fished forth the limp packet of smokes Galloway had given him, selected one, lit it and re-pocketed the packet as he spoke around a mouthful of exhaled smoke.

'From California, eh?'

Galloway was interested. 'What makes you think so?'

The fat man smiled, dug out the cigarette packet and pointed to the state tax stamp on it. 'California,' he said again, and settled back comfortably. 'I'll tell you what I think, fella; you're no more an aberrationist than I am. In my city we teethe on people like that, and after a while every cop gets to know the real types just by feel, by sight and feel. You're no more a queer than I am. So — why the disguise?'

'Maybe in Chicago you're tops,' replied Galloway, 'but in England you're a failure at reading people.'

The fat man turned and gave Galloway a hard appraisal, then stubbornly shook his head. 'That's no good, fella. I've been over here many times before and there just is not that much difference. I'll tell you what, fella, you level with me and if it's nothing big I'll overlook it.'

Galloway, who had held the initiative

up until now, had no intention of relinquishing it; if he did, if he allowed the big fat Chicago detective to obtain the upper hand, he might just as well resign himself to being manhandled by the big man when they landed in London. He leaned and said, 'Fella — you are about one big breath away from having eight inches of steel stuck between your ribs. We're still about an hour out. You relax and shut up all the rest of the way, or they'll take you off in London feet first.'

The detective instinctively looked down, but there was no knife in sight although Galloway had one fist hidden beneath the coat-lining on the detective's side of their adjoining seats. 'You should have stayed over where you were,' growled Galloway.

The stewardess came up taking orders for breakfast. She confirmed Galloway's opinion that they would be landing in an hour or less. She also gave Galloway a peculiar look because 'she' seemed to be fraternizing with that gross, particularly unattractive big man from across the aisle.

After they had ordered and the girl had

departed, the fat man put out his smoke, adjusted the seat to be back enough so that he could stretch out in comfort, and as Galloway decided he would now have to endure an hour of discomfort, pretending he had a knife inside the lining of his coat, the stewardess flipped on a television newscast to help dispell, or at least to help alleviate, the monotony which was now, finally, beginning to border on some kind of involuntary movement among all those restless people.

The news was not pleasant, but then Galloway could never remember when it had been. The best any news commentator could do was inject a little humour from time to time, but the bare facts of history-in-the-making were chilling, unpleasant, and full of imminent menace.

There were seven insurrections taking place, plus two furious little brushfire wars that seemed quite capable of sucking a lot of objecting people into their spheres, and even on the non-military side, the news was of labour strikes, postal threats of strikes, dock-workers and warehousemen threatening to tie up all the medicines being stored prior to delivery, by other strikes, and even some airline pilots were demanding more money or they would also leave their jobs.

Otherwise, a very mysterious and bizarre aircraft hi-jacking had taken place several hours earlier. A young revolutionary brandishing a home-made bomb filled with nerve gas, had forced an airplane bound for Caracas, Venezuela, to divert to Havana. The Cuban authorities were annoyed because the aircraft required re-fuelling before they could send it back to the U.S. They were also annoyed because the young man who had hi-jacked the aircraft was hopelessly insane; they had no use for *bona fide* revolutionaries, said the newscaster, who were a dime a hundred in the Caribbean nowadays, but for insane ones they didn't even have prison room. This one, according to the newscast, had been securely bound, handcuffed and chained, and had then been flung back inside the aircraft and went back to the Americans. Only one person had been removed from the aircraft; a passenger everyone was astounded to discover, when the Cubans insisted upon searching passengers, turned out to be a man disguised as a woman. The Cubans took a small fortune from this mysterious individual, said the newscaster, and escorted their unique prisoner away, refusing to release him to return to the United States along with the other passengers.

Galloway let all his breath out very slowly, and took down a big, fresh breath. And now, he asked himself, what became of Minden?

At his side the fat detective who had been ordered not to speak, broke the rule. 'Okay; by accident the pinkos in Havana knocked off one of you. Or was it an accident? Fella, all they have to do in London is find that you're also carrying a big fat money-belt, and you'll have had it.'

Galloway's temper flared but he controlled it. If, by putting up with the needling from the Chicago detective Galloway could reach London without trouble in the air, it might not be too exorbitant a price to pay. What troubled him was what he would have to do when they were about to land. Patiently, the detective was only going to wait until he was sure of reinforcements, then he was going to make some kind of move, probably a discreet one so that, if it turned out Galloway was nothing more than the aberrationist he was pretending to be, the Chicago detective would not be too humiliated.

Also, it seemed now that the Chicago detective did not really believe Galloway had a knife. It required no vast stroke of genius to guess that the detective knew all about those electronic weapons detectors airlines used, had known right from the start Galloway had no knife, and no gun either.

If there had been a way to reach Inspector Merritt by telephone from the airliner, Galloway would have considered making the call, but actually the idea of having to appeal for help did not sit too well with him. Whether Merritt had thought Galloway could bring off the re-theft or not, if Galloway could manage the entire episode by himself, it would look a lot better than if, at the last moment, he had to cry for help.

'What is it,' asked the fat detective, 'some kind of international conspiracy of tutti-fruitis — of mock Women's Liberation shock troops? Where does the next nut turn up, in London airport maybe?'

Galloway leaned back as though perfectly comfortable and relaxed, turned his head and said, 'I thought the idea was that you weren't going to talk until we landed.'

The fat man's thick lips drooped. 'Did you? Come off it, fella, I'm interested. You may not even be in any trouble, for all I know. But let's hear the bare-bones facts.'

Galloway thought, and gazed at the fat man, and finally decided in a perfectly cold blooded manner what he had to do. He had probably a half an hour yet before he'd have to do it, and in that length of time he had to decide *how* to do it without causing a furor aboard the airplane.

When he spoke to the detective,

though, he gave no sign that he had come to a decision. In fact, judging from his answer, it was more likely that he was more than ever in a quandry.

'The bare-bones facts,' he said quietly, 'are that the third world is rising up against both capitalists and communists, and the first victims are to be the police.'

The detective's expression hardened. 'Very funny, fella. Okay; you can play it your way, right up until we land. Then let's see which way the ball bounces.'

Galloway looked at his watch, looked up front where the armed guard was back now, but reading a newspaper and no longer paying any attention to the passengers, and decided that they were probably even closer to landing than he had thought.

The fat man sighed, shook his head and settled comfortably in his seat. 'You haven't got a prayer of a chance, fella. Maybe their plumbing isn't the best over here, but you ought to know, judging from your accent, that their police work is as good as any in the world.'

Galloway sat back, rolled his eyes, and

said, 'I'm sure they would be pleased to know you are satisfied that they have managed to achieve parity with the Chicago Police Department. That must be a great compliment, even though in London they haven't been able to kill any students yet, and therefore are still a little behind you people.'

The fat man's heavy face turned a splotchy red as his small, alert and malevolent eyes turned fiercely upon Galloway, who now leaned forward as though to remove his coat, and while in the act of doing that, swung viciously from the shoulder with a bone-hard fist that caught the detective flush on the point of his coarse chin, knocking his head back so violently the bolted seat groaned from stress. The detective turned limp and nearly slid off his seat. Galloway pulled back the shielding length of his coat and used one arm to prevent the fat man from sliding further.

There was one thin trickle of blood at the corner of the fat man's lips, which Galloway wiped away very quickly as he kept his back turned to the aisle to shield the fat man from anyone who might be interested enough to be watching, which became highly improbable because, quite suddenly, the aircraft suddenly lost most of its powerful, thrusting sound, and seemed momentarily to be floating in an eerie kind of silent vacuum as it began to let down, began to get into position for the long, earthward glide that would carry it inland over the villages, the pastures, the great estates, and ultimately, the endless row of identical slate and tile roofs of London.

Everyone, with two exceptions, craned out the portholes, and even when the little sign came on reminding everyone that their seat-belts had to be secured, so little attention was paid to it that the stewardess had to call people's attention to this regulation by using her loud-speaker.

Galloway had to let out the seat-strap to its maximum length to get it around the unconscious fat man. He also had to roll the fat man's head towards the wall, towards the bulkhead porthole, so that if the stewardess came, as she usually did, to make certain all the straps were fastened, she would not see the unmistakably blank and unconsciously vacant expression on the detective's face.

It was a terrible few minutes, some of the worst Galloway had ever spent, and although he was perspiring freely when he felt the aircraft turbines begin to pick up again, boosting the aircraft over the last tier of roof-tops, he also had a feeling of immense relief.

He had made it.

All he had to do now was get off the damned airplane before it was discovered, as of course it would be, and shortly after landing, too, that the man with whom he had been sitting, had been struck a savage blow that had rendered him unconscious, because the moment that was discovered there would be police swarming all over the aircraft and the airport.

It wouldn't help one bit that they'd discover that the unconscious man was an American detective, nor that his only companion had been a woman listed on the passenger list as Mary Louise Merritt of London.

22

Home is Where the Heart Is

Galloway retrieved his suitcase then went hurriedly in search of a ladies lounge to change before confronting the immigration people. He would have preferred using a men's room, but the chances of entering one dressed as a woman, without having an airport security officer come right in after him, was too remote, and too risky. Of course, when he had changed and emerged from the ladies lounge he got several double-takes too, but one way or the other he had to run this risk, either going in or coming out, and actually this did not trouble him as much as getting out of the airport building did, because even dressed as a man again, in his own comfortable attire, and with his face scrubbed to remove the last vestige of the disguise, he still felt uncomfortable. By now the fat detective from Chicago would be revived, angry as a hornet, and screaming his head off about a description of the man-woman who had assaulted him. The police would be looking for both a man *and* a woman.

Going through customs was not a very complicated nor prolonged procedure, ordinarily, but today it appeared that several airliners had landed at roughly the same time, from different parts of the world, and Galloway had to queue up like everyone else.

He saw several men he thought might be plainclothes detectives enter the large room and make a careful study of the lines, and Galloway hunched down a little, dropped his head and hoped for the best. Eventually, those men departed and for ten minutes Galloway was relieved, then he finally reached an immigration and customs official, answered the curt questions, got a keen, two-second look, and was waved on. Thereafter he could mix with the crowd heading towards a very wide set of metal steps, and go down to the lower level beyond which he could see the many doors leading to the street beyond. Galloway had the impression one sometimes gets in a dream of running furiously towards safety without actually being able to move out of one's steps. He willed the crowd to hurry, but it didn't because it was largely composed of people who had come to welcome friends and relatives, and everyone was talking at once while walking slowly.

Two uniformed policemen and a man in civilian attire cut in front of Galloway and very neatly cut out a young man on ahead like sheep dogs cutting out an alien ewe or wether. It was done so deftly that despite the obvious astonishment and protest of the young man, the police had him over to the edge of the crowd in moments. He was younger than Galloway, but otherwise he matched him in build and general appearance very well.

Then the doors were ahead, Galloway shot through them, straightened up and hastened towards the rank of cabs. He flung in the suitcases, barked his address, leapt in and as the cab lunged away into the noisy, furiously charging London traffic, Galloway sank back and closed his eyes for a moment to wait until the tumult inside his chest subsided. Then he relaxed, watched a lot of familiar landmarks blur past, and turned eventually, just out of commonplace apprehension and studied all the cars that were behind the cab. There may have been an unmarked police vehicle back there but he did not really believe that, so he sat forward again, braced when the cab nipped round a corner heading towards his flat, and finally, with his building in sight, began to realize that he had in fact actually made it.

He paid the cabby, loped up the stairs to his rooms, flung open the door and tossed the suitcase upon a sofa, then, regardless of the time of day, he stepped into the tiny kitchen mixed a stout gin-and-tonic, flung off his tie and jacket, strolled to his favourite chair and dropped down with the feeling of a labourer who has just reached home after a hard, and an honest, day's work.

Someone knocked on the door. He considered the noise and the door, then said loudly it wasn't locked, and Inspector Merritt filled the opening. Merritt nodded without smiling, closed the door after himself and came ahead towards a chair with that rolling, somewhat muscle-bound walk of his. He said, 'Welcome home, lad.'

Galloway raised his highball glass as a sort of returned-salute. 'You timed it exceptionally well, if you just guessed.'

Merritt lightly scratched the tip of his nose. 'As a matter of fact it wasn't quite a guess. I received the paintings in the morning post, which was extremely gratifying, but that had no bearing on my coming over here. It was a complaint filed by a gentleman named Reynold from Chicago that made me think you might have got home.'

Galloway drank deeply and propped both feet upon a nearby chair. 'Big fat slob,' he said. 'Police detective?'

Merritt nodded. 'The same.'

Galloway took another drink. 'Never heard of him,' he told Merritt, and the inspector did not look surprised.

'He told us a wild story about another man dressed as a woman being appre-hended in Cuba during an aircraft hi-jacking. He seemed to believe there was a connection between that person and the man dressed as a woman he detected on the overseas flight he was on — the same person, he avers, who caught him entirely off guard, and knocked him out on the airplane just at landing time, then made an escape. Sounds a little far-fetched, wouldn't you say?'

Galloway nodded. 'Definitely far-fetched. Has Inspector Reynold decided to drop it?'

Merritt nodded. 'He's left it in our hands, and we'll investigate of course. He'll be flying back to Chicago next week and will drop round for a report before departing. I'll personally see to it that he is told we are still investigating. Maybe someday, when Inspector Reynold retires, he can include this adventure in his memoirs. I understand it's a very dull American detective who doesn't write a biography after retirement.'

Galloway was not interested. 'Can I fix you a gin-and-tonic?'

Merritt declined. 'No thanks, I've just had breakfast. Just wanted to drop round and say I'm glad you're back.'

Galloway was not flattered nor particularly pleased. 'Any complaints?'

'None, so far. You didn't have to kill anyone, by some chance?'

'No. But the man in Cuba was involved, and although I'm confident I'll never see him again, there is a wealthy solicitor, Howard Bennison, in Beverly Hills — recipient of stolen art work — who may try to find me.'

Merritt wrote the name in a small notebook and pocketed it. 'I think we can look after Mister Bennison or anyone he sends round. Anything else?'

Galloway thought he knew what was in Inspector Merritt's mind. 'Such as?'

'Well; you did manage to secure recompense for your trouble, didn't you?'

'I got by,' said Galloway, guardedly. 'Are you probing, Inspector?'

'Not really, although I'm terribly curious. If the man in Cuba was relieved of a fortune, and you and he were in some way associated, was there very much left for you?'

Galloway finished his drink, looked at

his feet and changed the subject. 'Too bad about Mitreman, eh?'

Merritt understood. 'Terrible thing. But of course we both know criminals in America think in terms of murdering their victims.'

'This time the victim had it coming,' said Galloway. 'Odd thing about crimes involving a lot of money; criminal alliances become very vulnerable.' Galloway leaned to put his empty glass aside. 'In England or America, so I rather suppose human nature is the same.' Galloway arose. 'One question, Inspector: What do you tell the people at the art gallery when you return their paintings?'

Merritt heaved his great bulk up out of the chair before replying. He looked slightly apologetic, too. 'Well, as a matter of fact, the standard procedure is to return the objects and only mention in passing that recovery was accomplished through the expertise of the police department.' Merritt raised his eyes. 'Of course I owe you one, Galloway. I won't forget, although of course if you revert . . . ' Merritt left it unfinished and went back across to the doorway. 'Someday perhaps we can sit down over a bottle of sherry and you can tell me precisely how you managed it, eh?'

Galloway nodded. 'Some day, perhaps, Inspector. Close the door on your way out.'

After Merritt's departure Galloway went to bathe and change, and afterwards to re-count that American money he had brought back with him. There was the mild awkwardness of depositing it at the bank, but as a matter of fact it was much easier to deposit American money than it was to take it out of the country. As for the questions Galloway was certain to be asked, he thought he'd be able to answer adequately. Payment for services rendered, and if anyone chose to verify that or to question it, let them, Galloway would say just that much and no more. The money would not be reported stolen, then too, there was the remark Merritt had made, probably in an unguarded moment: ' . . . I owe you one, Galloway.'

As for the actual amount — Galloway straightened up from re-counting it, looked around his dingy flat, looked out a window where sunshine and noise in equal parts came up from busy daylight London, and recalled how, for most of his life, he had entertained a dream of *someday* owning one of those country cottages, perhaps with a thatched roof, but of course slate would be better. In either case, though, it had to be reasonably close to a village and a decent old-fashioned pub where a man could trek on rainy days in his overshoes and tweeds, light up and mingle with the locals.

Galloway smiled and stepped to the window. Down below people as thick as hair on a dog's back jostled one another in an atmosphere of exhaust fumes from cars and an incoming, slowly creeping clammy kind of river-fog. A stalwart police constable stood imperturbably upon a street corner looking in the opposite direction, and several American sailors swaggered past behind two sari-clad Indian women.

Galloway went after his jacket, shrugged into it, neglected the tie, scooped up handfuls of money and pocketed the stuff, and left his flat to go to the bank. Oddly enough, although he got a startled look when he counted out that American currency, nothing at all was said. In London people were sophisticated and discreet, and also they didn't give a damn. Afterwards, Galloway strode down to the restaurant where he normally ate, got a bland look of surprise from the proprietor, whom he had known for several years, and went to his usual table near the front window where he could have lunch and watch the panorama stream past at the same time.

The proprietor came over and took Galloway's order, then he said, 'You've been gone.'

Galloway nodded. 'Business trip overseas.'

The proprietor looked saddened. 'Unfortunate. Last week I had the finest beef roasts I've ever been able to acquire. Beautiful cuts.'

Galloway could afford to be philosophical about his misfortune and after the proprietor left he sat back to watch the stream of people. It was probably true, as someone had once said, that if a man sat on a busy thoroughfare in London or New York long enough, he would see everyone in the world go past.

A large, massive hulk of a man in a dark suit loomed up like a shark in a school of minnows. People broke around him as he came steadily onward. Galloway recognized the man at once, and when the fat man's head turned and their eyes met, the large man's gait faltered just for a moment. Galloway nodded, smiled crookedly, and let his gaze slide past. The big man, though, paused in the centre of the human stream, looking past the window. His expression showed doubt, wonderment, curiosity, and a hint of deep-down bafflement, as though he *thought* there was something familiar about the relaxed Englishman inside the restaurant, but also as though he was unable to be sure.

Galloway drifted his gaze back, met those puzzled grey eyes, and noted with some satisfaction that the big man had a slight discolouration along the lower part of his jaw on each side of his chin.

Galloway had the sore knuckles to match.

Then the big man gave up, finally, and moved on again. Galloway leaned to see if he stopped or if he kept on moving. He did not stop.

The meal arrived and Galloway's host served the coffee himself. Not every Englishman drank coffee, but when one did he usually had his own ritual about the stuff. Galloway was no exception, and after preparing it to his taste, he sampled it as though it were a French or Rhine wine. The proprietor waited, then smiled and moved off when Galloway sighed as he replaced the cup.

There were disadvantages to country life. Galloway tried to imagine a proprietor in some ancient stone village being as solicitous of his welfare, and failed. And there was something else too; it was commonly said that thatched roofs harboured every imaginable variety of spider and bug and creeping thing.

And of course there was the quiet and the unchanging serenity. Galloway looked out the window and saw a very handsome pair of swinging hips go by. Nothing like that in the villages.

He decided that somewhere over the recent years, the Galloway who had always wanted to live the quiet, serene, cottage-life, had died, leaving behind the Galloway who could steal a fortune in America, and come back to London where he belonged, without a scratch.

He sipped his coffee, waited for something else to swing past, and gradually felt like the old Morton Galloway again, the loner who belonged exactly where he was. And there were worse things, for a fact. A man named Minden could have borne that out, if he'd been able, and perhaps so could a man named Bennison, not to mention one called Martinelli.

Galloway resumed eating, and made one final concession to that other Galloway: He would take a week or two off and go tour the countryside, then come back to London, like a sensible man, and settle down again.

We do hope that you have enjoyed reading this large print book.

Did you know that all of our titles are available for purchase?

We publish a wide range of high quality large print books including:
**Romances, Mysteries, Classics
General Fiction
Non Fiction and Westerns**

Special interest titles available in large print are:
**The Little Oxford Dictionary
Music Book, Song Book
Hymn Book, Service Book**

Also available from us courtesy of Oxford University Press:
**Young Readers' Dictionary
(large print edition)
Young Readers' Thesaurus
(large print edition)**

For further information or a free brochure, please contact us at:
**Ulverscroft Large Print Books Ltd.,
The Green, Bradgate Road, Anstey,
Leicester, LE7 7FU, England.
Tel:** (00 44) **0116 236 4325**
Fax: (00 44) **0116 234 0205**

THE GIRL HUNTERS

Sydney J. Bounds

Doll Winters was a naïve teenager, who fantasised about being a film character. But when Gerald Dodd committed a brutal killing, she found herself starring in a real-life murder drama — as the star witness! And when Dodd tries to silence her, Doll turns for help to the famous private detective Simon Brand. Then a further terrifying attempt on her life forces her to go on the run. But can Brand find her before the killer can?